THIS TIME WON'T YOU SAVE ME 2

KYIRIS ASHLEY

URBAN AINT DEAD

Contact Publisher at www.urbanaintdead.com

Email: urbanaintdead@gmail.com

Print ISBN: 979-8-9904701-7-0

CONTENTS

<u>Soundtracks</u>

Scan the QR Code below to listen to the Soundtracks/Singles
of some of your favorite U.A.D titles:

Don't have Spotify or Apple Music?
No Sweat!
Visit your choice streaming platform and search URBAN
AINT DEAD.

Currently on lock serving a bid?
JPay, iHeartRadio, WHATEVER!
We got you covered.

Simply log into your facility's kiosk or tablet, go to music and
search URBAN AINT DEAD.

URBAN AINT DEAD

Like & Follow us on social media:
FB - URBAN AINT DEAD
IG: @urbanaintdead
Tik Tok - @urbanaintdead

<u>**Submissions**</u>

Submit the first three chapters of your completed manuscript to <u>urbanaintdead@gmail.com</u>, subject line: Your book's title. The manuscript must be in a .doc file and sent as an attachment. The document should be in Times New Roman, double-spaced, and in size 12 font. Also, provide your synopsis and full contact information. If sending multiple submissions, they must each be in a separate email. Have a story but no way to submit it electronically? You can still submit to URBAN AINT DEAD. Send in the first three chapters, written or typed, of your completed manuscript to:

URBAN AINT DEAD
P.O Box 448
Maybrook, NY 12543

DO NOT send original manuscript. Must be a duplicate.
Provide your synopsis and a cover letter containing your full contact information.
Thanks for considering URBAN AINT DEAD.

CHAPTER ONE

Aspen sat in the waiting room alongside Brianna as she watched Tonya pace the floor. Everyone's emotions ran rapid as they waited for the doctors to walk in the room and tell them any news on Justice's condition. She'd taken a turn for the worst in the few short moments that Brianna and Aspen had gone outside, giving the hospital a code blue alert. Dr. Michaels and her entire team were all in Justice's room, working on her. Silent tears fell from Aspen's eyes as she tried her best to keep praying. Her heart was heavy, and she felt as though everything around her was falling apart. Her best friend was in the hospital fighting for her life, while the woman who'd been like a mother to her had been kidnapped and was being held for ransom. *None of us were supposed to get hurt. We were supposed to protect each other. How the fuck did we let this shit happen?*

Aspen had so many different emotions running through her at once. She was hurt and afraid for Justice's life, not knowing if she would pull through or not. She couldn't imagine losing her friend and didn't even want to think about that happening. Aspen was also mad at herself for allowing this to happen. However, Aspen also knew the laws of the streets. She knew she couldn't choose how someone reacted after they'd taken all their money and their weight. She just wished they all could have gotten away from it unharmed.

They'd come up with a plan to get Shanté back themselves and use the money they'd stolen for Justice's surgery. Aspen just hoped they had enough firepower to do it alone. Aspen was afraid, but she knew it had to happen. She couldn't allow fear to get the best of her. They already didn't have the amount of money the kidnappers requested, and part of what they had needed to be spent on Justice's surgery. The only option they had was to go get Shanté themselves. She knew that if they didn't, whoever had her would indeed kill her. So, they would have to do everything in their power to assure that didn't happen.

After what seemed like hours, Dr. Michaels stepped into the waiting room to give the family an update.

"While we have stabilized Ms. Lewis, she is not out the woods yet. She desperately needs a kidney transplant, and we are now ready to test everyone that wants to be tested," she informed.

"Test me first! If I'm a match, my baby can have my

kidney. Hell, she can take them both if that means she's gon' live," Cream declared.

He didn't care what he had to do. He wanted to make sure Justice would make it out of this situation alive. Whatever the surgery cost, Cream was going to make sure that it was paid by any means. He loved Justice with all of his heart and couldn't imagine a life without her.

"Great. Someone will be out to get you shortly to test you," Dr. Michaels voiced.

"We all want to get tested," Brianna spoke up. She knew the more of them that got tested, the greater the chance was that at least one of them would be a match.

"I'm glad that she has this much support. Believe it or not, support from your loved ones does a lot for the recovery of a patient. Once everyone is tested, I can take you all to visit with her. We normally only allow two people in the room at once. However, I will make an exception and allow the four of you to go in together."

"Thank you, Doctor," Brianna spoke.

The doctor exited the waiting room, and they all waited for the nurse to arrive, so they could be taken to begin testing. Aspen's cell rang, and she immediately answered it, noticing it was Quan. She was in shambles, and he was the only one that could put her mind at ease.

"Baby, where are you?" Aspen asked as soon as she swiped the talk button.

"Just got to the crib. Where you at? I been missing you all

day," Quan spoke lovingly. Just the sound of his voice put strength back into Aspen, and she felt instant relief.

"I'm at the hospital. Justice got shot. It's not looking good for her right now. She needs a kidney transplant. We all waiting to get tested now."

"Damn, what hospital? Were you with her when she got shot?" he asked. Questions began rolling off his tongue like water, and Aspen couldn't answer them fast enough. She ended the call with Quan letting her know he was on his way to the hospital.

Cream was the first of them to go back to get tested. They informed him that the results would take about twenty-four hours before they came back. However, for an extra cost, they could put a rush on the results. He sat there, mind racing. The fear of possibly losing Justice forever was entirely too much for him. Justice was the love of his life, and he didn't want a life that didn't include her. He vowed to himself that he was going to find whoever was responsible for Justice's shooting, knowing that when he found them, he would kill whoever it was with his bare hands. *Justice don't deserve to be laid up in a hospital bed, fighting for her life. I swear I'm takin' the lives of everyone involved. I don't give a fuck who they are,* Cream thought.

Once everyone was finished being tested, they all walked back into the waiting room, waiting on the doctor to take them to see Justice. Both Quan and Loke were in the waiting area when they walked back inside. The girls were so happy to see their boyfriends that they both ran over and hugged them, needing the comfort they knew they would receive from them.

Loke walked over to Cream, giving him a few encouraging words, knowing that the situation had to be hard for him.

"How you holdin' up, bro?" Loke asked, already knowing the answer.

"I'm fucked up. I need for my baby to pull through and be okay. I swear I'm gon' kill whoever the fuck did this shit."

"Let me know what's up. Justice was cool people and Brianna's family, which makes her my family. So, if you wanna ride out fo' dis, I'll ride out wit' you," Loke informed.

"Good lookin', my dawg."

Dr. Michaels walked into the waiting room, informing them that they could come to see Justice. She motioned them to follow her as she led them down the hall, taking them back to Justice's room. When they entered, the sight before them broke all their hearts. She lay in the hospital bed, eyes closed and hooked to several monitors. There were tubes in her nose and mouth and an I.V. inside her hand, giving her medicine to keep her asleep. She was a mere shell of her former self, and none of them had prepared themselves to see Justice that way. Cream was the first one at her bedside, pulling up a chair to sit next to her as he grabbed her hand. He felt so helpless as he had to put the life of his woman in someone else's hands. He couldn't understand how something so tragic could happen to someone so loving. Justice was one of the good ones, and Cream knew she didn't deserve what was happening to her. *I need to talk to Aspen and Brianna because the story of how this happened ain't adding up to me,* he thought.

Tonya sat on the opposite side of Justice, tears flowing freely from her face. Seeing her daughter this way was heartbreaking. "I'm so sorry, baby," Tonya whispered.

Aspen and Brianna stood off to the side, not knowing what to say or do. Deep down, they both knew they were to blame for what happened to Justice. *We should have stopped this shit the first time,* Aspen thought. As much as she wanted to beat herself up about what was going on, she knew doing that wouldn't make things better. They had to take matters into their own hands when it came to Shanté while praying that the doctors could save Justice.

Dr. Michaels gave them an hour with Justice before letting them know that only one person could stay with her throughout the night. When both Cream and Tonya refused to leave, Dr. Michaels sympathized, allowing them both to stay. Aspen and Brianna kissed Justice on the forehead before saying their goodbyes to Tonya and Cream.

"This shit is fucked up, B. Our girl is laying up in a hospital bed, not knowing if she gon' live or die. They took Shanté and is doing God knows what to her. I'm not tryin' to act gangsta or nothing, but I feel like blowin' this whole city up 'bout dem," Aspen whispered as they walked down the hall.

"Yeah, I get it. I feel the same way. We need a plan. We

already don't know who we dealin' with. I can't have neither one of us getting hurt too," Brianna replied.

"We going in that bitch guns blazin'. That's the plan. Shit, it ain't like we ain't never bodied a muthafucka before. Any fear I had went out the window the moment I saw Justice laying in that bed with all them tubes. Ms. Shanté can't be next."

Brianna nodded her head in agreement. There was no way she was going to let anyone hurt her mother for something she did. "Do you think we should tell Loke and Quan what's going on? Shit, Cream too. I know if we did, they would help us. We might need them behind us," Brianna suggested.

Aspen thought for a moment. There was no question that her man would have her back. She just didn't know if she wanted to involve him in her drama. She knew Brianna was right though. They might need them. With that, she agreed they should let them know what was going on and allow them to help.

ASPEN WALKED INSIDE HER HOUSE WITH QUAN RIGHT BEHIND her. She walked upstairs and headed directly to her room, removing her bloody clothing. The last few days had taken a toll on Aspen, and she hadn't realized how much until that moment.

"I'm going to run you a bath," Quan suggested, grabbing

her vanilla scented bubble bath off the dresser and heading into the bathroom.

Aspen stood there, naked, thinking about the many hours they would have to wait before they found out if any of them were a match for Justice. *What if none of us are? What the fuck will we do then?* The doctor had informed them that a transplant was the only way Justice would live. *My best friend can't die*, she thought to herself, dropping her head low. Tears began falling from her eyes uncontrollably as she fell to the floor. She had been trying to be the strong one this entire time. However, as she sat there in the middle of her bedroom floor, her emotions had gotten the best of her. Quan, hearing Aspen crying, came back into the room, immediately sitting down beside her and wrapping his arms around her.

"It's okay, baby," Quan whispered, kissing Aspen on her forehead.

"It's not okay. This is too much, and it's all my fault," Aspen cried.

"How is this your fault? You didn't do anything to make this happen," Quan reassured, not wanting Aspen to blame herself.

Aspen felt ashamed to take the conversation any further, but she knew she had to. When they had first started hitting licks, she never thought that things would end this way. They had made millions in their prime and were living life to its fullest. However, Aspen didn't think the short-lived fun was worth the heartache of what was taking place. She attempted to lock eyes with Quan before she spoke but dropped her head before she could get the words out.

"This is my fault, our fault, all of it. I'm not who you think I am, Quan." Her voice was trembling, and she fiddled with her fingers, trying to come up with the words to say.

"What do you mean?" Quan asked, placing his pointer finger under Aspen's chin and lifting her head up, so they could look each other in the eyes.

"The three of us been hittin' licks the last few years. That's how I get my money. We been hittin' different stash houses and takin' them fo everything they had. Shit was working for a long time, bringing us hella money. Shit was coming so fast that none of us wanted to stop."

Quan didn't speak; he just listened, taking in everything she was telling him. He wanted to make sure he heard every-thing clearly before he responded. So, he gave Aspen his full attention as she laid her secrets out on a platter.

"Did Justice really get shot in a drive by, or did it happen while y'all was hittin' a lick?" Quan asked.

"The drive by really happened, but I'm pretty sure it was somebody that we hit a lick on that did it."

"And Bri's uncle?" Quan asked.

Aspen hung her head low as tears continued to stream down her face. "I'm sure that was somebody we hit too. We fucked up bad, Quan.

"Before Justice got shot, somebody kidnapped Ms. Shanté and wants ten mill to get her back. That's the reason we was out there like that for the drive by to even happen," she continued.

"So, do you think the same people that got Shanté is the people that shot Justice?" Quan was trying to get as much detail as he could from Aspen. He wanted to know everything so that he wouldn't go into anything with a blind eye.

"We not sure, could be. Me and Bri came up with a plan to go get Ms. Shanté back from them without paying them the ten million that we don't have. We don't know nothing about them though, so I was thinkin' that you can come with us. You know, just in case shit gets outta hand."

Quan nodded his head, running his hand over his face. Aspen could tell he was in deep thought, and she only hoped that he would ride for her the way she would for him. She prayed that he would still love her even after she'd revealed her true self to him.

"I'ma always ride for you, baby. I got you on anything you need. What time is the drop?" Quan questioned, showing Aspen he was down for whatever.

"They gon' call us tomorrow with a time and place. I don't know how dangerous these people are, but it's clear they ain't playin' no games 'bout they money."

"We got it. I don't give a fuck who they are. They gon' learn real quick that I don't play no games 'bout you," Quan spoke. He looked Aspen in the eyes before he continued.

"Don't ever think you have to hide anything from me. You been dealing with all this shit alone when you could have had my shoulder to lean on. As your man, it's my job to make sure you good, but you gotta let me do that. I got you, baby, so let me have you."

Quan kissed Aspen on her forehead before pulling her into his tight embrace. Aspen melted into his arms, glad that he, indeed, had her back. The love she felt for Quan was different from any other man she'd been with. Aspen looked into Quan's eyes and knew she was looking into the eyes of her soulmate. No matter what the future held, Aspen no longer feared it, knowing Quan would be by her side.

Aspen's phone rang around nine the next morning. She was already awake after not getting much sleep the night before. However, she was still lying in bed. She swiped the talk button and answered. Realizing it was the hospital, informing her that she was a match for Justice, she jumped up out of bed, letting them know that she would be there within the hour. Rushing into the bathroom, she quickly took a shower. Once she was done washing, she placed a call to Brianna, putting her on speaker as she dressed.

"What up doe?" Brianna answered.

"The hospital just called me. I'm on my way up there now. Did they call you?"

"No, I haven't gotten a call. What did they say?" Brianna asked.

"They told me I was a match for Justice. This means she gon' be okay."

"Oh, thank God. I'm gonna get dressed real quick and meet you up there," Brianna screeched.

Aspen agreed before ending the call. After she was dressed, she informed Quan that she was on her way to the hospital. She let him know that she was a match for Justice and would probably be going into surgery. She kissed him goodbye with Quan letting her know he was getting dressed and heading to the hospital. Aspen walked out the door, making her way to Sinai Grace Hospital.

When Aspen arrived, she parked her car and called Brianna, wanting to get her ETA. When Brianna informed her that she would be pulling up in five minutes, Aspen decided to wait on her. Brianna spotted Aspen's G-wagon as soon as she pulled into the parking lot, and she parked next to her. They both got out their cars and walked into the hospital. When they got up to the ICU, they walked to the desk and asked for Dr. Michaels.

"They called y'all too?" Cream asked, walking up to them.

"Yeah, they called me. Brianna came up here with me."

"I never left. I can't leave her up here like that. They did tell me that I wasn't a match though. But I'm glad to hear that you are," Cream stated.

"I'm a match too," Tonya spoke, walking up and joining them at the desk.

The group watched as Dr. Michaels walked up to them. She greeted them all with a smile.

"I'm glad to see you all are here for Justice again. As you all know, we have run tests on all of you, trying to find a match for Justice. I am happy to say that we did find two matches for her. Both Ms. Billups and Ms. Lewis are good matches. Although both of you are matches for Justice, in my professional opinion, Ms. Billups being the younger of the two might be a better option."

"Then let's get to it," Aspen announced, not giving it a second thought.

Dr. Michaels nodded her head and instructed both Aspen and Tonya to follow her. They walked down the hall and into a smaller room. They took a seat and listened to Dr. Michaels explain to them how they would have to each take a pregnancy test before they went any further.

"Oh, well, I'm good there. My tubes been tied for the last ten years," Tonya informed.

"That may be true, but we still have to follow proper protocol. Once the results of the tests come back, we can go from there. It should only take a few minutes."

Dr. Michaels handed them both a small cup with their names written on it before directing them to the bathroom. When they were done, they walked back inside the room and waited on Dr. Michaels to reenter. Walking back into the room about ten minutes later, Dr. Michaels took her seat, reading over a few papers before she began speaking.

"Like I've stated moments earlier, a pregnancy test is required for women to assure we don't do anything that might harm an unborn child. Aspen, although you are a great match, you will not be able to donate your kidney at this time. Your pregnancy test has come back positive."

If Aspen wasn't already sitting down, she would have fell to the floor. Pregnant was the last thing she thought the doctor would say. She'd thought she'd been very careful with Quan, always making him use a condom. Now she was realizing that she hadn't been safe enough. Here she was, a perfect match to save her friend's life and couldn't even do so because she was pregnant. She could see Dr. Michael's lips moving but didn't hear anything after the word pregnant.

"But I'm still a match though, right? We can still use my kidney to save my baby?" Tonya questioned, wanting to know what was going to happen next.

"Yes, Ms. Lewis. We will get you prepped and ready for surgery within the hour," Dr. Michaels informed. "Ms. Billups, congratulations on your pregnancy. I hope this news brings joy to you and your family."

Aspen nodded her head but didn't speak. She was still in shock after finding out she was pregnant. *Bitch, you can't think about this shit right now. You still got way too much shit to do. Get Ms. Shanté back first, make sure Justice is good, then you can focus on your pregnancy,* Aspen thought. She knew the moment she told Quan she was pregnant, he would make her sit down. There was no way she could leave Bri on stuck and not help her get Ms. Shanté back. The pregnancy had already prevented her from helping to save Justice. So, she decided to wait before she told anyone.

She made her way back to Justice's room where Brianna and Cream were both sitting. Aspen didn't know what she'd just walked in on, but it seemed as though they were in deep conversation. She took a sat in a chair next to Justice's bed. She was still in the medically induced coma and looked to be sleeping so peacefully. Aspen was all over the place. She knew she had business to take care of, but all she kept hearing in her head was Dr. Michaels telling her she was pregnant.

"Ain't that right, Aspen?" Brianna called out.

"Yeah, um, huh? Wait, what you say?" Aspen asked, stumbling over her words. She didn't even know Brianna was saying anything to her until she heard her call her name.

"I said the people that took my mama could be the same people that shot Justice."

While Aspen was in the back, finding out why she couldn't donate her kidney to Justice, Brianna had let Cream in on everything that was really going on. Aspen had been in such a daze after finding out the news that she didn't hear what they were talking about when she walked into the room. When she looked up at Cream's face, she could see his anger.

"Aspen, I asked you to tell me what happened." Cream spoke through clenched teeth.

"And I did. We don't know who shot at us. It could very well be the people that kidnapped Ms. Shanté, or it could be someone else. We don't know. Hell, we don't even know who got Ms. Shanté."

"Fuck!" Cream yelled. "Why the fuck would she be hittin' licks with y'all? Justice didn't have to do that shit. She knows I would take care of her and give her anything she needed or wanted. She made good money with her businesses too. Why the fuck would she do that?" Cream questioned, not understanding why Justice would risk her life for money.

"I know it might seem crazy to you, but Justice was addicted to the money. It was coming so fast, and she was spending it even faster," Brianna informed.

"Yeah-fuckin-right! Justice had money; she made her own. If she was hittin' licks, it's cause y'all needed money, and she was trying to help y'all. Justice was good."

Aspen had had enough. She knew Cream's emotions were running high. However, so were everyone else's. There was no way she was going to allow Cream to stand there and paint his own narrative. "Nah, you not 'bout to do that shit. We all were out there hittin' licks, yes. It was times that we all wanted to. But it was also times that Brianna and I didn't want to but still did because we couldn't let Justice hit them by herself. Look, Cream, I know it's hard finding out you didn't know Justice like you thought you did, but this shit hard on us all. Justice is

Brianna's cousin and my best friend. We want her to pull through just like you do. Then, on top of that, Brianna's mother was kidnapped. Oh, and let's not forget they shot the car up that we were all in. Justice might have been the only one that got shot, but they was gunnin' for us all. We don't know who wants us dead. So, you gon' have to calm that shit down," Aspen continued.

Cream nodded his head. "You right. My bad. I'm all over the place with this shit, and it got a nigga fucked up. I ain't mean to come at y'all like that."

Aspen nodded her head and gave a half smile, letting Cream know that she understood. She knew he was under a lot of stress, so she wasn't going to hold his words against him.

"When do you go into surgery?" Brianna asked.

"I'm not. Ms. Tonya gon' do it." Aspen shrugged, not wanting to take the conversation any further.

"But I thought Dr. Michaels said you were a better choice?" Cream pressed.

"Yeah, well, that was before they ran other tests and real-ized Ms. Tonya was the best choice. Justice is getting a kidney though, so that's all that matters. Now, we need to figure out what we gon' do 'bout Ms. Shanté."

"Loke said he would help with whatever I needed," Brianna informed.

"Yeah, Quan said the same," Aspen revealed.

"Just text me the time and place when y'all find out. When they supposed to be callin' y'all?" Cream inquired.

"Shit, I guess sometime today. The note they left said we had seventy-two hours. But when they called yesterday, they said they would call today," Brianna uttered.

"Just let me know. I need to find out myself if they had anything to do with Justice being shot." Cream took Justice's hand into his before he continued. "Cause whoever did this to her gon' get theirs. I promise."

CHAPTER TWO

*J*ustice had been wheeled out of her room and taken to surgery. Cream had come up with more than half of the money for the surgeries and the testing, and Brianna and Aspen gave him the rest. By that time, Quan had made it to the hospital, and they were all sitting in the waiting room. Dr. Michaels had already informed them that the surgeries would take several hours, so all they could do was wait.

"Y'all want something from the vending machine? I need some water or something. My mouth dry as hell," Aspen uttered.

Both Quan and Cream declined, while Brianna opted to come with Aspen. They both walked down the hall in search of a vending machine. "I hope everything is going okay with the surgery," Brianna voiced, letting out her worry.

"They said Dr. Michaels is the best doctor at this hospital, so I'm sure she has it under control. Justice gonna be up and getting on our damn nerves again before you know it," Aspen joked.

"Yeah, you right. I'm just ready for this shit to be over."

After grabbing their drinks, they made their way back to the waiting room. It had only been an hour since Tonya and Justice had gone back for surgery, but it felt like forever to everyone else as they waited.

SHANTÉ FOUND HERSELF CHAINED TO THE SAME CHAIR IN THE basement yet again. Only this time, she knew exactly who had her. Yet she still had no idea why. She'd almost gotten away when she was caught and taken right back to the musty basement. She didn't know what Lashay wanted with her but planned to find out the moment she walked down the stairs.

"Damn, I was so close to getting the fuck outta here. How the hell did I let them get me again?" Shanté spoke out loud.

She had managed to get out of the chains once and felt she could do it again. All she needed was a chance, and when it came, she was definitely going to take it. Shanté was determined to live and make it back to her daughter, and she vowed to do just that. She looked around the floor for the makeshift shank she'd had. However, she quickly realized that she'd dropped it upstairs trying to get away. She heard the door open and footsteps coming down the steps toward her.

"Bitch, why the fuck am I here?" Shanté yelled the moment Lashay stepped into her line of sight. Shanté didn't understand why Lashay had any smoke with her. *She's the one that came in spilling secrets that ruined my life. I should be the one that kidnapped this bitch.*

Lashay looked down at Shanté as if the mere sight of her disgusted her. Lashay hated Shanté. She had for years. In her eyes, Shanté was the reason her life had taken a turn for the worst. Just looking at Shanté brought back so many bad memories.

Summer 2004

LASHAY SAT AT THE VANITY IN HER BEDROOM AS SHE APPLIED a thick coat of dark brown liner to her lips. She swiped her lips with clear lip gloss before pressing her lips together, giving her color an ombre effect. She placed her hair into a high pony and pin curled it into a bun before flat ironing her two side bangs. She rubbed herself down with her Sweet Pea body lotion before putting on a blue camo crop top and a pair of dark denim capri pants. Once she slid her huge hoop earrings into her ears and sprayed the same Sweet Pea body spray all over herself, she was dressed. Now, she waited. Ant had called her and told her to get dressed, and Lashay didn't hesitate to do so.

Lashay turned on her radio, and Beyoncé sang, prompting Lashay to sing along. "Looking so crazy in love. You got me looking so crazy in love," she sang as she danced in her mirror, watching herself with every move. Her phone rang, and she rushed over to it. She knew it was Ant, and she pressed talk before placing the phone to her ear.

"I'm outside," he spoke smoothly into the phone.

"Here I come, Daddy." Lashay beamed before ending the call. Walking down the stairs, she saw her mama in the living room, sitting on the couch. She had a box of Newport cigarettes sitting on the coffee table next to her glass of vodka and cranberry juice. Lashay's one-year-old twins, Malaysia and Maliki, sat on the floor in front of the TV, watching whatever cartoon Lisa had on for them.

"Where you going?" Lisa asked, looking up at her daughter. She had just gotten off her sixteen-hour work shift. It was Saturday, and she knew her fifteen-year-old daughter wanted to hang out with her friends. However, she wasn't going to allow her to leave her in the house with her children all day. Lisa knew all too well about being a teenage parent, having had her first child at the tender age of thirteen. Lisa's mother never helped her with her children, even going as far as kicking her out when she got pregnant. So, she vowed to be a different mother than she had. Although she couldn't break the generational curse of having children early, she was definitely breaking the curse of the non-loving mother.

"I'm 'bout to go to Northland with some friends," Lashay lied, not wanting to tell her mother she was going out to see a boy. She figured if she told her mother where she was really going, she wouldn't want to watch her kids, so she lied.

Lisa nodded her head before letting Lashay know to be home by eight o'clock. Lashay agreed, kissing her twins on their foreheads before rushing out to Ant's car. She was trying to hurry in case her mother looked out the window.

"You smell good," Ant complimented, kissing Lashay on the cheek.

"Thank you," she cooed. Lashay loved being around Ant. At just fifteen years old, she was smitten with the young hustler. She'd met Ant a few months prior when she was walking to the corner store. He pulled up alongside her in his dark green Buick Regal and offered her a ride. Lashay was instantly attracted to him as she looked at his smooth dark skin. His hair was neatly braided straight back, and the jewelry around his neck and wrist let her know he was getting money. She accepted the ride and had been seeing Ant ever since. In her mind, Ant was her man, but Ant would never so much as claim Lashay as more than his friend. At eighteen, Ant was a few years older than her and only looking to have fun. Everyone in the hood knew Lashay was easy. Lashay was a hoe, and all the guys in the hood knew what she was working with. Regardless to who Lashay was, Ant wasn't ready to be tied down to anyone. He was never the type to kept his eggs in one basket. So, being in a relationship with Lashay was a no go.

Ant pulled up to his apartment building, and they both got out the car. Once inside Ant's apartment, Lashay took a seat on his couch, grabbing the remote and turning on the TV. Ant grabbed his weed tray, sitting next to Lashay as he rolled a blunt. He lit it, puffing it a few times before handing it to Lashay. He knew the weed always brought out the freak in her, and he needed that. Ant watched the way she wrapped her lips around the blunt and imagined how it would feel when she put those same lips around his dick.

"Take yo' clothes off," Ant ordered once Lashay handed the blunt back to him.

Lashay smiled, standing up from the couch and removing her shirt. She ran her hands over her white lace bra and cupped her breasts while winking at Ant. She tried her best to be seductive, taking the blunt from him, smoking it as she unzipped her capris. Ant watched her every move, his manhood stiffening as she removed each article of clothing.

She stood before him in her matching panties and bra set, winding her hips as Ant watched her. Pulling his manhood from his pants, he stroked it as he motioned for her to come closer. She followed his orders, dropping to her knees in front of him, taking him into her mouth. She sucked and slurped, preforming the art of dick sucking like no other. Lashay alternated between sucking his dick and licking his balls, knowing exactly what Ant liked. He was in Heaven as he moaned out in pleasure.

"That's right, baby. Suck that dick fa' Daddy. Do that shit like you love this dick," Ant panted.

Lashay took all of him into her mouth, causing the head of his shaft to touch the back of her throat. "Damn, baby. You gon' make this muthafucka bust before I get to feel some of that wet pussy," he continued.

"Ain't no rush. We got plenty of time to do both," Lashay whispered softly, licking up Ant's shaft slowly as she looked into his eyes.

"Nah, I need some of that good shit right now." Ant pulled himself from her mouth before standing to his feet. Lashay already knew what was up as she bent over the couch, assuming the position.

Ant placed the tip of his manhood onto her wetness and closed his eyes before entering her all the way. Her love was so tight and wet that Ant thought he would explode with every pump. Lashay screamed with each backshot, matching Ant's rhythm as she threw it back. She loved the way he filled her up, and she wished he could stay inside her forever. They said that sex and love weren't the same thing; however, Lashay knew that what she was feeling for Ant was much stronger than lust. After about ten minutes, Ant could no longer hold his nut. Her wetness had him going crazy as he gripped her hips tightly and increased his speed. Before he knew it, Ant was releasing himself inside of Lashay.

Ant went right to the bathroom, grabbing a towel to clean himself with. Lashay was next, going to the bathroom and cleaning herself up before putting her clothes back on. She sat on the couch, putting her feet up, before grabbing the remote. She flicked through the channels, trying to find a movie they would both like. When Ant reentered the room, he was fully dressed with his shoes on.

"Come on. I'm takin' you home," Ant spoke, grabbing his keys from the coffee table.

"Home? I thought we would chill for a minute. Maybe watch a movie or something."

"Nah, I ain't got time to chill. Let's go," Ant ordered. He'd gone to pick up Lashay for one reason and one reason only. Now that he'd gotten his nut, it was time for her to go.

Lashay looked up at Ant sadly as she put her shoes on her feet. She'd just sucked his dick like never before, and he was ready for her to go? She'd thought they would spend the day together, watch a few movies, maybe order some food. Him making her leave after they'd just fucked had her feeling a type of way.

"Why don't you ever want to spend time with me?" Lashay asked.

"What you mean? We just spent time together. Fuckin' is the closest two people can be. I just gave my body to you. That don't mean nothing to you?"

Lashay knew that sex with Ant was good. However, she wanted more than just sex with him. She wanted to go on dates and spend Saturday afternoons at his house. She wanted to let the world know that Ant was her man, and she didn't understand why he didn't want to do the same.

"Baby, don't you think we should start spending more time together? Normal boyfriends don't fuck they girlfriends then send them home."

Ant recoiled before bursting out into laughter. "What the fuck are you even talking about? We not boyfriend and girlfriend. We have fun, yes. I like you and everything, but we not in a relationship nor will we ever be. I'm not ready for no relationship right now," Ant spoke.

"Boy, stop fronting. Who fuckin' and suckin' on you the way I am? If I'm not yo girlfriend, then who is?"

Ant just shook his head. It was almost like Lashay wasn't listening to what he was saying. He'd told her repeatedly that they were not in a relationship. Ant knew that he would never be with Lashay but would fuck her for as long as she allowed him to. *I know this bitch don't think I could ever take her seriously. She fifteen with two kids already. I could never wife her. Bitch got more bodies on her than one of them hoes standing on Woodward.* "Let's go, Lashay," Ant ordered, walking out his front door before Lashay could say another word.

When Ant pulled back up to Lashay's house, she got out of his car without even saying goodbye. She was a bit salty because of Ant dropping her off so fast. She went right into her room, lying across her bed.

"I'm gon' show that nigga. He ain't gonna keep using me for sex."

A NT MADE HIS WAY TO THE EASTSIDE, PULLING UP AT HIS brother, Darius' house and parking in his driveway. Before he could knock on the door, it swung open, and Shanté came rushing out. Tears were streaming down her face.

"Shanté, you good?" Ant asked.

She looked up at him with tear filled eyes and broke down before she could speak. Ant instantly became nervous, pulling his gun from his waistline, not knowing what was going on. "Where is Darius?" Ant asked, fearing the worst.

"Who knows? Probably somewhere cheating on me as usual," Shanté shot back.

She had been with Darius for the past two years, and he'd cheated on her more times than she could count. She truly loved Darius but hated the way he treated her. "Why he keep doing this shit to me, Ant? He knows I love him. These other bitches don't give a fuck about him. They just want the money that comes with him. But he gon' hurt me to fuck with them?" Shanté cried.

Ant didn't know what to do or say. He'd never seen a female cry so hard before, and the sight broke his heart. He placed his gun back into his waistline and wrapped his arms around Shanté, hugging her tightly. "It's gonna be okay.

Darius loves you too. He just don't know how to show that shit right now. Y'all gon' be cool though."

Ant tried his best to calm Shanté down, but it didn't seem to be working. She seemed to be crying harder as he held her in his arms.

"I just don't understand why he's doing this shit to us. I treat that nigga good. I fuck him when he wants to be fucked. I suck him when he wants to be sucked. I do it all, so why would he even want anyone else? Them bitches don't care about him. All them hoes see is dollar signs."

Ant was a man, so he knew how women threw the pussy at him. Bitches saw the car you drove and the jewelry you wore and saw money. So, of course they wanted to fuck you. It was hard to stay faithful when you had your pick of pussy to choose from. Ant understood wholeheartedly; he just couldn't tell Shanté that. Ant and his brother, Darius, had gotten in the drug game during their early teens, and it had brought them a lot of money. One thing about those gold-digging bitches was they would always chase a nigga with money.

"Look, Shanté, I know Darius might fuck around with different bitches from time to time, but that don't mean he don't want to be with you. I know he loves you, but sometimes the temptation can be overwhelming. He's young and so are you. He will come around eventually and realize you are all he needs," Ant assured.

Shanté looked up at Ant, nodding her head as she wiped her

tears. She truly loved Darius. He was her first everything — first boy she kissed, first boy she loved, and the first boy she had given her body to. She wanted their relationship to work. She wanted to be able to tell people years down the line how they were childhood sweethearts and had stayed together, beating all the odds. So, she decided she wouldn't let another bitch take away her happiness.

"Thank you, Ant. I really needed that talk." Shanté smiled.

Ant watched as Shanté walked away, heading down the street. Ant walked inside Darius' house, pulling out his cell phone to call him. "What up doe?" Darius answered.

"Bro, where you at? I'm at yo crib, and Shanté was here on ten. Fuck you do to her, bro?"

"Man, she trippin'. She went through my phone and saw some shit she ain't wanna see. I asked her why she would go through my phone, and that shit set her off. I had to leave my own house to cool shit off."

"Man, when I pulled up, she was walking out. She was cryin' so damn hard that I ain't know what the hell was going on. Shit, I thought someone had came in and did something to you the way she was actin'."

"I'm 'bout to come home. I'll be there in 'bout five minutes," Darius informed.

THE FOLLOWING DAY, LASHAY CALLED ANT, WANTING HIM TO come get her. He'd planned to sit and enjoy the football game over a couple of beers. However, when Lashay offered to give him one of her famous blow jobs, he agreed to pick her up. Within the hour, he'd picked up Lashay and was now back at his house. He turned on the game and rolled a blunt. He took several pulls before passing it over to Lashay.

"Ant, are we ever gonna be together?" Lashay asked, looking over at Ant. She wanted to see the look in his eyes when he answered the question.

"Why do you want to be in a relationship so bad? Why can't shit just be good the way it is? I'm not trippin', so why are you? You still get to see me when you want, right? So, why you tryin' to fuck with a good thing? I feel like you got more important things to think about than being in a relationship with me or anyone else."

"Yeah, but who else gets to see you? Who else do you let fuck and suck on you? And what else do you want me to think about other than you? I love you, Ant, and I just want to be with you. You keep acting like it's just sex between us when you know we are so much more than that. We already act like we together, so why not just be together?" Lashay asked.

"Ain't no way you love me, Lashay. We are literally just fuckin'. See, this is exactly why we not in a relationship. You over here asking questions that don't concern you now. If we was in a relationship, I could only imagine the shit you would be trying to ask. You got two kids already. They who you should be thinkin' 'bout."

"So, you are fuckin' somebody else?" Lashay asked.

"I think it's time for you to go. Come on. I'm 'bout to take you home. I'm not 'bout to do this shit."

"What? What are you talking 'bout? I thought we was chillin'," Lashay questioned in confusion. She didn't understand why he wanted to take her home now. Lashay wanted to have this conversation. She wanted Ant to want to have this conversation as well. *How can this nigga not want to be with me? I'm good enough to fuck but not good enough for a relationship? And now he wants to send me home? Man, fuck him.*

"You know what? Fuck this. You can just take me home," Lashay snapped, standing to her feet before gathering her belongings.

"That was happening anyway," Ant shot back. He opened the door and watched Lashay as she stormed out. He dropped Lashay off at her house, pulling off before she even walked inside.

Ant had had enough of Lashay. *Bitches always gotta fuck up a good thing. Damn, she had some good ass pussy too,* Ant thought as he drove down the street, heading back home. He grabbed a beer and sat on his couch, watching the game, as soon as he got home. He had just grabbed his third beer when he heard a knock at his door. Looking out the peephole, he noticed it was his brother and opened the door.

"What up doe, bro?" Ant greeted, allowing his brother inside his home.

"Shit, I was coming over here to see what you had going on," Darius replied.

"I ain't doing shit. Sitting here, watching the game. You want a beer?"

"Yeah, I'll take a cold one."

Darius took a seat on the couch and watched the game with his brother. "What's up with you and Lashay? How y'all been?" Darius asked.

"Man, I just had to take that bitch home. She talkin' that relationship shit, but I ain't wit' it. I told her from the jump what this shit was about, and she was wit' it. But you know how bitches always think they can change a nigga and shit."

"Yeah, that be the bullshit right there. I love my girl; you know I do. But sometimes, I wish I would have waited to get in a relationship. It be so many bitches throwin' pussy at a nigga, and I be wantin' to sample that shit. But it seems like every time I do, Shanté always finds out. Then we into it."

"See, and that's what I don't want. This my dick, and I want to do what I want with it without worrying 'bout somebody getting mad or being hurt. But it seems like Lashay just wasn't gettin' that shit," Ant informed.

"I feel that. But Lashay a freak hoe anyway. You can't make that bitch yo girl no way," Darius responded.

"I don't want to make her my girl, but that bitch had some dawg ass pussy. I might have to double back and hit that shit one more time before I really let her go for good." Ant laughed.

CHAPTER THREE

Shanté had just gotten her license, and as a congratulatory gift, Darius bought her a Nisan Altima. Shanté couldn't have been more excited about her first car. It was dark blue with tinted windows and twenty-inch rims. She loved the car and made sure to give Darius the proper thank you.

One winter's night, Shanté decided to take a drive over to Darius' house. He had been hustling hard for the past week, and they had barely spent any time together. Her mother was working the midnight shift at Oakwood Hospital, and her brother was gone. Shanté wanted to spend the night with her man, and that was exactly what she was going to do. She pulled up to Darius' house, smiling when she saw his Jeep in the driveway. She was happy to see her man was at home and not in the streets with the next bitch.

She got out her car, eager to jump into her man's arms. She made her way up the walkway joyfully, quickly walking up the steps. She was just about to knock on the door when she glanced through the front window. The curtains were wide open, making it easy for her to look directly inside the house. The sight before her almost sent her to her knees. There, sitting on the couch, was Darius, and on top of him, riding him like he was her own personal stallion, was Shanté's cousin, Peanut.

Shanté was fully aware of her cousin's hoe status around the hood. She would fuck anybody that said hello to her. She'd gotten into several fights, both at school and around the hood, for fucking on other girls' boyfriends. Some of those fights, Shanté even had to help her win. She would have never thought that Peanut would do her dirty and fuck Darius. Most importantly, she would have never thought that Darius would go so low as to fuck her cousin.

She watched as Darius picked Peanut up, standing to his feet and bending her over the couch, putting her in the doggystyle position without even taking his dick out of her. Shanté didn't know what to do as she stood there, watching with tears streaming down her face. She walked back down the steps, getting into her car and pulling off before they even knew she was there.

"How could this muthafucka do some shit like that to me? He's supposed to be my man. He tells me he loves me every day, but he goes and fucks my cousin?" Shanté spoke aloud as she drove down the street. When she got back home, she went right to her room, crying in bed for the rest of the night.

Shanté woke up the next morning feeling like her heart was broken into tiny pieces. She lay in bed, staring at her TV. A movie was on, but all she saw was the visions of Darius fucking the shit out of Peanut. It was Saturday morning, and normally, she would be getting dressed to go to the mall or to get her nails done. However, after last night, all she wanted to do was lay in bed.

Her cell phone rang, and she didn't even bother to look at it. She didn't care who it was because she didn't want to talk to anyone. She had never felt this type of pain before and didn't know how she was going to get over it. It felt as if her entire world was coming to an end, and there was nothing she could do to stop it. When her phone rang several more times, she finally looked at it. When she saw it was Darius, she turned her ringer off. She had nothing at all to say to him, and she knew that anything that came out of his mouth regarding the situation would be a lie. Shanté had seen it with her own eyes, so there was nothing she needed to hear from either of them.

That following day, Shanté decided that she would get up and take a shower. *I ain't 'bout to let them keep me sad. I'm going to the mall to get me a new outfit for school tomorrow,* she thought. She grabbed her vanilla scented body wash and headed to the bathroom. Her mother was at work like she normally was, and she had no clue where her older brother was. At sixteen years old, Shanté was practically raising herself. There was rarely any adult supervision due to the long hours her mother worked. When she wasn't at work, she was either sleeping because she'd just gotten off of work or she was getting ready to go to work. There were no days off for a single mother who needed to pay all the bills and provide for her children. So, Shanté came and went as she pleased. As long as she showed up to school every day, she could do whatever she wanted.

Once she was dressed, she got in her car and headed to Northland Mall. She needed a way to clear her mind, and she thought that shopping was the exact way to do so. She went in store after store, trying on tons of clothes and shoes, purchasing everything that she wanted. Shanté was at the mall for several hours before she decided to get herself something to eat. Walking inside the food court, she went right to the Chinese spot and placed an order. Once she had her food, she went and took a seat at a table, ready to enjoy her orange chicken. The time she was spending with herself was much needed, and she hadn't thought about Darius since she'd been at the mall. When she was finished eating, she went right back to shopping, spending a few more hours at the mall before going back home.

Shanté put all of her new clothes and shoes in her closet. When she was done, she went down to her living room and turned on the TV. She was sitting on her couch, flicking through channels, when she heard a knock at the door. Before she could get up, her brother, Mook, opened the door. Peanut walked into the house, smiling from ear to ear.

"Shanté, what up doe? I been callin' yo ass. Something wrong with yo phone?" Peanut asked, walking up to the couch.

Shanté rolled her eyes, not wanting to be bothered with Peanut at all. "What do you want?" Shanté shot back.

"Damn, what's wrong with you, cousin? Let me find out that nigga done did somethin' to you. I'ma fuck his ass up."

Shanté looked up at Peanut, dumbfounded. *This bitch got some nerve comin' in my fuckin' house, talking to me like she wasn't just throwin' it back on my fuckin' man like he was the last nigga on Earth. This bitch better get out my face before I fuck her ass up.*

"That nigga, Darius, better get his shit together cause I'll smile in that mugshot 'bout you, cousin," Peanut continued.

"Girl, get the fuck out my face."

"Huh? What you say?" Peanut asked in confusion.

"I said get the fuck out my face. Bitch, you standing here talking to me like we cool or some shit when yo slutty ass was just fuckin' on my man. You lucky I didn't blow yo shit out the moment you walked in my door."

Shanté stood to her feet, walking up in Peanut's face. She was ready to beat her ass right there on the spot. Her emotions were all over the place. Seeing Peanut face to face made rage shoot throughout her body. She balled her fist up tightly, ready to throw a punch at the first lie she told.

"Shanté, I don't know what that nigga told you, but I am not fuckin' no damn Darius. Why the fuck would I fuck yo man, Shanté? You my cousin. I would never do that shit to you."

"Bitch, don't try to play me like I'm fuckin' dumb. You a fuckin' hoe. You literally fuck everybody's man. I thought that since you were my cousin that you would have some fuckin' respect. But I see I was wrong. Get yo dirty, dusty ass the fuck out my house, bitch, before I fuck you up."

"Wow, so you gonna believe an outsider over me? I ain't never fucked Darius, and whoever told you that is a fuckin' liar. The fact that you would even believe them says a lot about you," Peanut shot back.

With those words, Shanté cocked back and bust Peanut right in the mouth. She was sick of her standing there, lying, and was going to show her that she didn't play those games. Peanut screamed as Shanté laid punch after punch down on her. She tried to fight back but was no match for the anger that was running through Shanté. Mook, hearing the commotion, came running in from the kitchen, grabbing Shanté and pulling her off Peanut.

"Yo, what the fuck is wrong with y'all? Why y'all in here fighting like y'all ain't fuckin' family?" Mook shouted.

"Fuck this bitch! She ain't no fuckin' family of mine. This bitch been fuckin' my man behind my damn back. Ain't no tellin' how long she been doing that shit. She just a fuckin' hoe!" Shanté screamed, trying to get close enough to Peanut so she could hit her again. Mook was holding Shanté tightly, not wanting her to fight in their mother's home.

"Shanté, I told you I didn't fuck him. I'm yo family. You should believe my word over anyone's."

"Bitch, I saw you with my own two eyes. Get yo lying ass out my house and don't ever fuckin' come back here."

Peanut walked out the door without saying another word. She knew she'd been caught, and her relationship with her cousin would never be the same again. Shanté ran up to her room, grabbing her keys and her coat before walking out the door. Her heart was crushed as tears streamed down her face. *Why the fuck would she come here? You gotta be one snake ass bitch to fuck yo people's man then come sit in their face like nothing happened,* Shanté thought as she tried to wipe her fallen tears. She needed something to calm her down, so she decided to drive to Ant's house and buy a bag of weed from him. She needed to smoke so that she could at least get her thoughts together and relax.

She pulled up to Ant's apartment building just a few moments later and got out the car. She walked up to the second floor before knocking on his door. *Damn, I probably should have called him first. What if he has company? What if Darius is here?* Ant opened the door, stunned to see Shanté on the other side. He stepped to the side, allowing her entry.

"What's up, Shanté? What brings you by?" he asked in confusion.

"I need some weed," she answered weakly.

"Darius out or something?" Ant took one look at Shanté and could see something was wrong. He could tell by the look in her eyes that she'd been crying, and he genuinely wanted to know why.

He walked into his kitchen, opened his cabinet, and pulled out a huge Ziplock bag full of weed. He reached his hand inside and pulled out a handful of buds, placing them into a separate smaller bag. Then, he handed the bag to Shanté.

"Here you go, Shanté. It's on me," Ant spoke, letting her know she didn't have to pay for the weed.

"Thanks, Ant."

Shanté sat on Ant's couch and pulled a grape White Owl from her purse. She began breaking down the weed before twisting it up into the cigar. Ant watched in confusion as she hit the blunt and took a deep pull.

"Shanté, what's up? Is something wrong? I mean, you're welcomed to smoke here; that's not what I'm saying. It's just weird that you smoking here."

Shanté looked up at Ant as huge tears ran down her face. Her heart was broken, and no matter how many pulls she took from the blunt, it didn't ease her pain. Ant saw the tears and knew that she was hurt by something Darius had done. He walked to his kitchen and grabbed a bottle of tequila and two shot glasses before sitting next to Shanté. He poured two shots before handing one to her. She took the shot, placing her glass onto the coffee table before she spoke.

"I saw Darius fuckin' Peanut."

"Damn, Shanté, I don't even know what to say." Ant was Darius' brother, and he would never speak bad about him to anyone. However, Ant knew that Shanté was one of the good girls, and he just couldn't understand why Darius treated her the way he did. Everyone knew that Shanté would do anything for Darius, no matter what it was. She was down for him; however, Darius treated her like she was just the average bitch. He could see the hurt in her eyes, and he wished there was something he could do to fix it.

"Shit is fucked up, ain't it? Out of all the bitches he could have fucked in Michigan, I would have never thought that Peanut would be one of them. This nigga literally has no respect for me."

"How did you catch them?" Ant asked, pouring them both another shot that they downed in seconds.

Shanté told the story about how she saw Darius fucking Peanut, and Ant couldn't do anything but shake his head. *Damn, this nigga sloppy as fuck. Why the hell didn't he take that hoe to a damn hotel? Peanut thick and shit, but she fo' everybody. I would have never risked that shit,* Ant thought. He watched as Shanté poured them each another shot. She took hers before pouring herself another.

"I just don't understand where things went wrong. I love him so much. But he still chooses to fuck with these raggedy ass bitches that don't give a fuck about him. Why am I not good enough for him, Ant?" Shanté cried.

"Nah, hell nah. Don't ever let nobody make you think you

not good enough. You are a wonderful person, and if people can't see that then it's they problem."

"Thank you, Ant." Shanté smiled. She was happy that she'd come to his house and gotten an ear to listen to her and some encouraging words.

"Anytime, Shanté." Ant wrapped one arm around Shanté, bringing her in for a half hug. Shanté wrapped both arms around Ant, hugging him tightly. She kissed his cheek gently, thanking him for making her feel better, slowly letting go of their embrace. She looked into Ant's eyes, and for a moment, the thoughts of why she'd picked the wrong brother ran through her mind. Before she knew it, they were sharing a passionate kiss.

Shanté placed her hand onto his crotch, feeling his rock-hard manhood. She became moist as she rubbed it. She knew what she was doing was wrong, but she couldn't stop herself. Her emotions were all over the place, and all she wanted was for the hurt to go away. Shanté wanted to feel good again. She didn't know if Ant could make that happen, but she for damn sure was going to see.

Ant began to unbutton her shirt, never breaking their kiss. Her lips tasted sweet and felt so soft that Ant didn't want to stop kissing her. He took her bra off before placing a trail of gentle kisses from her lips to her breasts. She moaned softly when he placed one of her nipples into his mouth. He sucked one as he softly twirled the other one in his fingers, causing

Shanté to throw her head back in ecstasy as her eyes rolled into the back of her head.

"Take your clothes off," Shanté whispered.

Ant obliged, standing to his feet and removing his clothes. Shanté looked up at him, admiring his naked body. She scooted to the edge of the couch and took his hardness into her mouth, sucking and slurping him like a lollipop.

"Damn, that shit feels good," Ant moaned. He gently stroked the side of her face as he looked down at her. She looked so sexy sucking his dick that Ant had to remove himself from her mouth in order not to bust. Picking her up, she wrapped her legs around his waist as he carried her to his bedroom. He laid her onto the bed as he slid her jeans off her body. He stood there, looking at her, and she took off her panties, letting him know that she wanted the exact same thing as he did.

Ant tongue kissed her belly button before trailing his tongue down to her love box. He rested his head between her thighs as he savored the sweet taste of her. Just eating her pussy had Ant mesmerized. Her soft moans sounded like music to his ears, and he continued to lick her just so he could hear them.

"You taste so good," Ant moaned in between licks.

"I want to feel you inside of me," Shanté urged.

Ant climbed on top of her, easing his manhood into her tight wetness. She moaned as he entered her and so did he. The way her walls felt around his dick made him think she was made for him. He pumped in and out of her slowly as she tightly wrapped her arms around him. Neither of them thought about the damage they were doing as they continued to please each other. When they were done, Shanté went home, feeling better than she did when she arrived.

THAT NEXT MORNING, ANT WAS AWAKENED BY SOMEONE beating on his door. Not knowing who it was, Ant grabbed his gun before making his way to the door.

"Who the fuck is it?" Ant called out as he made his way to the door.

"Bro, it's me. Open up."

Ant heard Darius yell, and he unlocked his door, opening it so that he could enter.

"Bro, I done fucked up," Darius said as soon as he walked inside.

"What you mean you fucked up? What happened?" Ant asked. He already knew what was going on, but he couldn't tell Darius that.

"I fucked Peanut, and Shanté found out. I have no clue how she knows, but she knows."

"Peanut? As in Shanté's cousin, Peanut? Why the fuck would you do some shit like that?"

"Man, I was thinkin' with my dick. She so fuckin' thick and damn near threw the pussy at me. I told her no a few times, but that last time, I just couldn't help myself."

"How you know Shanté knows?"

"Peanut told me she beat her ass when she went to her house. Shanté won't answer none of my calls or none of that shit. She gon' leave me, bro, and I can't let her go. Why the fuck did I do this stupid shit?"

"Damn, bro, this is fucked up. I know you been cheating on her for a while but to fuck her cousin? That's wild, even for you."

Ant walked over to the couch and grabbed his weed tray off his coffee table. He rolled a blunt and lit it before he continued.

"I ain't tryna kick you while you down or nothing like that, but what you gon' do?" Ant questioned, genuinely wanting to know the answer.

"I got to get her back. I can't just let her go like this. I love her, and I need her in my life. I know I fucked up, but I can't just let her walk away. Not like this." Darius dropped his head low. He'd never feared anything in his life, but he feared losing Shanté.

Ant looked into his brother's eyes and swore he saw tears in them. He knew Darius loved Shanté. He just didn't understand why he would do something so foul to her. He saw how good Shanté treated his brother, and he wished he had a girl like that in his life.

"Go to her house and talk to her. If you in her face then she has to listen," Ant suggested.

"You know what? You right. I'm 'bout to go over there

now. Thanks, bro." Darius agreed before walking out the door. He rushed to his car, making his way to Shanté's house. He didn't want her to leave him over this. No matter how many women he had sex with, Shanté was the only one he truly loved. She was down for him, and none of those bitches he fucked was as down as her. *Shit, I done fucked up.*

Darius did eighty miles per hour down the lodge, trying to make his way to Shanté. He wanted to show her that his love was only for her. He only hoped that Shanté would hear him out.

"You always gettin' us in trouble," Darius yelled, looking down as he grabbed his dick.

He knew he needed to learn to think with his head and not his dick. However, he didn't know if he could. Darius was still young, and that was something he didn't think Shanté understood. Even though he knew his heart wanted to be with Shanté for the rest of his life, his dick had other plans. He just wanted Shanté to know that just because he fucked another female, it didn't mean he loved them. Shanté was the only girl that had his heart, and he wanted her to know that. Darius was wrong when he fucked Peanut, knowing that family was off limits. So, that was what he would apologize for.

Darius pulled up in front of Shanté's house and knocked on the door. All he wanted to do was talk to her and let her know how sorry he was. When Mook answered the door and told him Shanté wasn't home, Darius stood there, dumbfounded, as he wondered where Shanté could be. He was walking off the porch, ready to get back in his car, when Shanté pulled in her driveway. Darius smiled, happy to get the chance to finally have a much-needed conversation with her.

Rushing over to her car, Darius tried to open her driver's door, but it was locked. "Baby, can I please talk to you?"

Shanté just looked up at him. She really didn't want to hear anything he had to say, but she knew he wouldn't leave her alone until she listened. "What's up?" Shanté asked, opening her door and getting out the car. "You got five minutes."

"Baby, look, I know I fucked up, and I'm sorry. I don't know why I did that shit. It was stupid, and I'm sorry. All I want is for us to get through this shit. I don't love her. I don't love none of them bitches. You are the only one I love. I want us to be together forever, baby. Please forgive me," Darius pleaded.

"I don't know, Darius. The shit is still too fresh. Even if I was to forgive you, it definitely wouldn't be right now. I'm tired of you cheating on me, and the fact that you fucked my cousin shows me that you have no respect for me. I can't deal with that. How can you even fix your lips to tell me you love me when you can't even respect me enough not to fuck my family?"

"Baby, I got nothing but respect for you. I want you to have my kids and be my wife. I don't give a fuck 'bout none of them other bitches."

"Then why Peanut? Out of all the bitches you could have

fucked, why would you fuck her? Was that the only time, or y'all been fuckin'?"

Darius dropped his head low, not ready to answer the question he was just asked. The truth was that Darius had been fucking Peanut twice a week for the past six months. He didn't want to tell her that, but he didn't want to lie to her either. He was trying to get her back and knew that would be hard to do if he told her the truth. However, he knew that if he lied and she found out, it would be over for sure. So, he did the one thing he never did with Shanté. He told the truth.

"We been fuckin' for a few months. She made the first move, but I won't put it all on her because I clearly ain't do shit to stop it. But, baby, I promise you I ain't touched her since you found out, and I ain't fucking her again. All I want is you," Darius replied.

Shanté just nodded her head. She couldn't believe they had been sleeping together for so long. She thought back on everything that had happened in the past few months, every time Darius told her he loved her, and every time she hung out with Peanut. *Damn, these muthafuckas really not shit,* she thought to herself.

"Shanté, where does this leave us?"

"I don't know," Shanté responded before walking away and going in the house.

CHAPTER FOUR

It had been two weeks since Lashay had last spoken with Ant, and she knew today would be the day she did. She'd found out two days ago that she was pregnant, and she couldn't be happier. Although she was only fifteen and this would be her third child, Lashay thought that the news of them having a child together would bring them closer than ever.

"We gon' be a family." Lashay smiled as she rubbed her stomach.

Lashay put on her coat and took the short walk to Ant's apartment. She thought about calling first but quickly decided against it. She feared he would hang up the phone before she would be able to tell him. However, she knew that if she was in his face then he would have to listen to her.

When she arrived at Ant's apartment building, she walked

inside and headed up to his apartment. She was all smiles as she thought about the way Ant would respond to the news of them becoming parents together. She knocked on his door, eager for him to open it. It had been weeks since she'd seen him, and she missed him tremendously.

"What are you doing here, Lashay? And why the hell didn't you call first?" Ant chastised as soon as he opened the door.

Lashay was caught off guard at the response she'd gotten. She'd expected him to welcome her with open arms after not seeing each other for so long. She smiled at him, trying to stay in good spirits as she attempted to walk inside. Ant quickly stood in front of her, stopping her from walking into his house.

"I asked what you were doing here?" Ant asked again.

"Ant, stop playing. I came to talk to you, babe. I haven't seen you in a while, and I miss you. Plus, I have a few things I need to speak to you about." Lashay chuckled, feeling a bit embarrassed that Ant wasn't happy to see her.

"Okay, then speak. Whatever you want to talk about could have been done over the phone."

"So, you saying I can't come in?" Lashay asked, now feeling hurt by his coldness.

"Either you tell me what you want or you get away from my door. I'm not playing these games with you. We not fucking with each other no more, so I really don't know why you even here."

Lashay nodded her head, clearly seeing that Ant wanted

nothing to do with her. She knew once she dropped the bomb she had that all that would change. So, she let Ant know exactly why she was there.

"I'm pregnant," she revealed, smiling from ear to ear.

Ant recoiled. He had no clue why Lashay was standing at his door, telling him all of this. Over the last couple of weeks, he'd started spending more time with Shanté. As horrible as it was for him to have feelings for her, he'd started to really like his brother's girlfriend. Shanté was the total opposite of what Lashay was, and something about Shanté made him want to be with her. He loved the time they spent together, even if it was in secret.

"I don't know why you telling me that shit. Lashay, you know damn well that I ain't yo damn baby daddy. I remember you had two other niggas thinkin' they was the father of yo twins before you found out it was a whole other nigga. Yo ass ain't 'bout to have me out here lookin' crazy," Ant spoke, the harshness in his tone cutting through Lashay's heart like a knife. "Get the fuck from in front of my door with that bullshit. You would say anything to try to trap me. Yo rat ass probably ain't even pregnant!"

Tears began to form in Lashay's eyes as she listened to Ant. She would have never thought that he would act this way toward her, and it was crushing her entire soul. She truly loved Ant, and she thought the moment she told him they were about to be a family that he would love her too. However, she was now realizing that things were not going to work out that way.

"Ant, you're the only person I been fuckin' with. I am definitely pregnant, and it is your baby. I just want us to be a family and raise our child together." Lashay was hurt, and her voice cracked as she spoke. She tried to fight the tears that were threatening to fall, but she lost that battle. Tears began streaming down her face as she looked into Ant's eyes.

"You thought we would do what? Let me make something clear to you right now. Me and you will never be family. If you really are pregnant then I will drive you to the clinic and pay for you to get that shit taken care of. That's as far that this shit gon' go. You think you can trap me? Hell nah! You the last person I want to have a baby with. So, like I said, hit me up when you make the appointment to get that shit taken care of," Ant continued.

"You know what? Fuck you! I don't need you to do a fuckin thing for me or my baby. Ain't nobody tried to trap you, fool. You the one that put yo dick in me. I ain't force you to do shit! And by the way, that little dick and the five minutes of sex you give ain't worth none of this!" Lashay shouted before storming off.

Tears fell as she walked down the hall. She was hoping that when she turned around, she would see Ant. She hoped he would come and get her, hug her, and tell her he was sorry. She wanted him to say they would be a family and that he would do anything he could to take care of her and their baby. However, instead, when she turned around, all she saw was Ant's closed apartment door. With a broken heart, Lashay exited Ant's apartment building and headed home.

SHANTÉ GOT IN HER CAR AND TOOK THE TWENTY-MINUTE drive out to downtown Dearborn. She was going to meet Ant for lunch, and they wanted to meet outside the city. They didn't want anyone that knew Darius to see them and tell him. Shanté walked into the restaurant and immediately spotted Ant. She walked up to him, and he stood to his feet, bringing her in for an embrace.

"You smell good," Ant complimented.

Shanté thanked him before they both took their seats. The waiter walked over, taking their drink orders before giving them time to look over the menu. After about ten minutes, the waiter was back and taking their orders. They sat together and enjoyed a wonderful lunch, engaging with each other like they were in an actual relationship.

"You want to go back to my apartment?" Ant asked.

"There's no other place I'd rather be," Shanté cooed.

Shanté followed Ant back to his apartment, parking down the street from his building, not wanting her car to be spotted. Shanté knew what she was doing was wrong; however, she'd been done so wrong by Darius that she just didn't care. Ant had been there for her in her time of need. Although she knew they could never really be together, she liked Ant and loved spending time with him. She knew it was going to be short lived, so she was going to savor every moment.

"You wanna smoke?" Ant asked once they walked into his apartment.

Shanté nodded her head yes, taking her shoes off and making herself comfortable. She watched as Ant twisted up a blunt before drying and lighting it.

"What time you gotta be home?" he asked, taking a long pull from the blunt.

"My mama works midnights, so I'm chilling. What time you got yo other bitch coming over?" Shanté joked.

"I let that bitch go, so it's only you." Ant smiled.

Shanté looked into his eyes and saw the truth in them. She smiled back at him before leaning over and kissing him softly.

"If you tell me you ready to do us, I'ma make that shit happen," Ant whispered.

Shanté was lost, stuck somewhere between the fairytale of being with Ant and the reality of loving Darius. If she knew Darius would treat her right and never cheat on her again, she would be with only him. However, she knew that was something he couldn't promise. So, for the moment, she would live in the fantasy of being Ant's girl, to feel the love and pleasure he gave only to her, even if it was morally incorrect.

Shanté didn't say anything in return. Instead, she continued to kiss him passionately, allowing her tongue to do the talking. There was a firm knock at the door, stopping their kiss abruptly.

"I thought you didn't have no bitches that would be coming over," Shanté whispered.

"I don't. I don't know who the fuck this is."

Ant stood from the couch and walked to the door. He looked out the peephole, and his heart dropped. He turned around quickly, mouthing to Shanté that Darius was at the door. Her eyes widened as she quickly jumped to her feet. She moved around frantically for several seconds, trying to figure out what to do. Finally, Ant told her to go into his bedroom and close the door. Once she was inside, Ant opened the door.

"What up, bro? What you doing here?" Ant asked.

"I gotta get my baby back. She the best thing that ever happened to me. I can't let nobody else feel that. I fucked up. I know I did. But I want her to know that I'm done with that shit, bro." Darius spoke in one breath.

Ant saw the look on his brother's face, and he knew he was devastated. The pain of losing Shanté was all over him, and it broke Ant's heart, even more so because Shanté was sitting right in his bedroom.

"Have you talked to her at all?" Ant asked, already knowing the answer.

"She won't say shit to me. I've tried calling over and over, but she won't answer none of my calls. I tried going to her house, but every time I do, she's not home. What if I really lose her this time?"

Ant was taken aback by how emotional his brother was. If Ant didn't know any better, he would have thought Darius was about to cry. Ant knew that Darius loved Shanté; he just didn't know he would react this way over losing her.

"I bought her this promise ring and everything. I just haven't seen her to give it to her," Darius said, pulling a small, velvet box from his pants pocket.

"You wanna marry her?" Ant asked, not believing his eyes. He stared down at the diamond ring before looking back up at his brother.

"This is just a promise ring. This is me promising her that it's just gonna be me and her from now on. I want to show her that I can be everything that she needs. I just need for her to let me," Darius continued.

Shanté stood on the other side of Ant's door, almost in tears as she listened to Darius speak. He was saying the words she always wanted to hear, and it broke her heart. Here she was, about to have sex with his brother, while Darius was out buying her a ring. She felt low and wanted nothing more than to run out there and jump into Darius' arms. However, she knew she couldn't. If she walked out now, Darius would want to know why she was in Ant's bedroom. She knew nothing she said would be able to explain that, so she stayed in the room, listening, until they were finished.

When she finally heard Darius leave, she walked out of Ant's bedroom. They both knew it was time for her to go home, and what was understood didn't need to be explained. She walked to the door with Ant right behind her. She turned to say goodbye, and Ant brought her into his embrace.

"In a perfect world, we would have been perfect for each other," Ant whispered.

"Why does this feel like goodbye?" Shanté asked, a single tear running down her cheek.

"Because it is. When you walk out that door, you go back to being what you always have been, my brother's girlfriend."

Shanté looked deep into Ant's eyes before kissing his lips. They stood there for several moments, holding each other for what they knew would be the last time, before Shanté rushed out the door, not looking back.

CHAPTER FIVE

A week had passed since Shanté had last see Ant, and she'd decided to take Darius' call. He asked to take her out to dinner, and she agreed, setting up a date for Friday night. Since she hadn't seen him in a while, she knew she would have to be dressed to the nines. She wanted him to see what he was missing and almost gave up. She started off by looking in her closet. She'd just gone shopping and had several items with tags still on them. After going through everything and realizing nothing gave what she wanted it to give, she decided to go to the mall.

Friday night came, and Shanté was in her room getting dressed. She'd skipped school earlier that day and had gone and gotten her hair and nails done. She was sitting at her vanity, applying her makeup, while listening to music. Her mother was at work, and her brother, Mook, was somewhere around the hood. Like most of the time, Shanté was at home alone. She dressed in a black, leather mini skirt that she paired with a black, halter top and matching leather jacket. It was cold in the city, but she looked damn good and knew it wouldn't be cold inside the restaurant. There was a knock at the door, and she knew it was Darius. So, she made him wait for several seconds before she finally went to open the door.

"Damn, you look good as hell," he complimented.

Shanté smiled, thanking him before walking out and getting into his car.

"I hope you're in the mood for seafood because I made reservations at Fish Bone for us," Darius informed.

"You know I'm always down for lobster and crab legs."

The two made their way to the restaurant where they shared a lovely dinner. Darius spared no expense, allowing Shanté to order ever item she wanted to try.

"Baby, I want you to know how sorry I am. I don't know what the fuck was going on with me, but I want you to know that shit is over. All I want is you. I want it to be me and you for life," Darius revealed.

He reached into his pocket and pulled out the small ring box. He placed it on the table and slid it over toward her.

"What's this?"

"Open it and see," Darius suggested.

Shanté, already knowing what it was, reached for the box. She opened it, and her eyes widened at the princess cut, diamond ring she was staring at.

"Now this is not an engagement ring, but it is a promise ring. This is me promising to do the best I can at never hurting you again. I know I fucked up, and I won't pretend like this is anyone's fault but mine. But I don't want to lose you. I'm willing to do anything to show you that."

Shanté looked into Darius' eyes and saw the sincerity in them. Her heart belonged to him, and she wanted nothing more than to be with Darius. However, she didn't know if she could trust that he wouldn't cheat again. The last time had crushed her, and Shanté knew she couldn't handle that type of pain again.

"What you did really hurt me. I'm not even cool with Peanut after what happened. I will take your ring, Darius, but if we do this again, it's gon' be at my own pace. I have to make sure my heart is protected. So, it's going to be rules. Starting with no sex. You have given your body to a lot of people other than me. And I need to make sure we build our emotional connection up before we even think about being physical again."

Darius looked at Shanté, clearly not liking what she was saying. However, wanting her back more than anything, he agreed to her terms. They finished their dinner before Darius dropped Shanté off at home.

ANT LAY IN BED, TOSSING AND TURNING. HE COULDN'T SLEEP at all, and the only thing that was on his mind was Shanté. He wanted to hear her voice and see her face. Rolling over, he looked over at his clock and noticed it was two fifteen in the morning. He knew it was too late to call Shanté, knowing she would probably be sleeping. He decided to send her a text just to let her know that he was thinking about her. To his surprise, Shanté texted right back, letting him know that she was thinking about him as well.

Do you want some company?

Ant stared at the text message for a few seconds. He wanted Shanté to come over; he needed her to come over. He just didn't want to hurt his brother the way he knew he was doing. Going against everything he stood for, Ant texted her back and told her to come over.

Twenty minutes later, Shanté was knocking on Ant's door. He opened it, quickly wrapping his arms around her and pulling her into him.

"I missed you so much," he whispered.

"I missed you too," she responded.

Ant began kissing Shanté passionately. He picked her up, and she wrapped her legs around his waist. He walked her to his bedroom where he laid her down on his bed. He undressed her slowly before resting his face between her thighs. She moaned in pleasure the moment his tongue touched her. They made love for the remainder of the night before falling asleep in each other's arms.

. . .

OVER THE NEXT SEVERAL WEEKS, SHANTÉ NAVIGATED HER time between Darius and Ant. Although she still wasn't having sex with Darius, she was getting it in with Ant on the regular. Her heart was torn between two brothers, and she had no clue what to do. The more time she spent with them both, the more torn she was. She'd just gotten out of the shower and was getting ready for school. Her mouth started to water, and she started feeling hot. She instantly felt like she had to throw up. Before she could make it to the toilet, Shanté was throwing up all over the bathroom.

"Damn, sis, what the fuck you eat? You sick or something?" Mook asked, yelling from the hallway.

"I don't know what is wrong with me. I just got sick out of nowhere," Shanté replied, walking out the bathroom.

"Yeah, Tonya got sick one day out of nowhere. Now Justice will be here in about four months."

"Shut up, Mook. You the only one 'bout to have a baby around here. I'm not pregnant."

Shanté spoke the words from her mouth; however, in the back of her mind, she wasn't really sure. She thought back to her last period, and she realized it was a bit abnormal. *It was only three days, and it was light as hell. Damn, am I pregnant?* She decided she would go get herself a pregnancy test just to make sure. So, after school that day, she went to CVS and purchased two tests.

When Shanté got home, she was happy to see that no one else was there. She ran up to the bathroom and took both tests.

She didn't have to wait the five minutes to get her results. It seemed as though as soon as she peed on the stick, she saw the two lines. *Fuck, I am pregnant. What the fuck am I gonna do?* She knew she wasn't pregnant by Darius since she had only been having sex with Ant for the past few months. *I can't tell Darius that I been fucking his brother. What will Ant even say once I tell him I'm pregnant?*

That Saturday morning, Shanté called Ant and asked if they could meet for lunch. She wanted to tell him the news face to face so that she could see his reaction with her own eyes. Once he agreed, Shanté dressed and headed out to Westland to meet Ant at their favorite restaurant. She walked inside and joined him at the table where he was already sitting.

"I'm glad you wanted to meet. I ain't gon' lie. A nigga was missin' you."

Shanté smiled, letting Ant know she missed him as well. The waiter walked over to the table, taking their orders before walking off to put them in. Shanté looked into Ant's eyes, not knowing how to tell him the news. Her heart began beating fast, and her palms started to sweat as she got nervous.

"Why you looking at me like that? What's wrong?" Ant asked.

"I'm pregnant," Shanté whispered, speaking in a lower tone than she intended.

"Wait, what did you say? Because it sounded like you said you were…"

"Pregnant," Shante spoke, finishing Ant's sentence.

The biggest smile spread across Ant's face as he stood up and walked around the table. He bent down in front of Shanté before wrapping his arms around her. "You're pregnant with my baby?" Ant asked, already knowing the answer. He knew Shanté hadn't been having sex with Darius, so he was the only possible father.

"Yeah."

"Hell yeah!" Ant yelled out loudly, causing the entire restaurant to look over in their direction. Ant didn't give a damn about the attention he was drawing to himself. He was excited about being a father and even more excited about the baby being by a woman he was in love with.

LASHAY STOOD IN THE WINDOW OF THE RESTAURANT WITH tears in her eyes. She watched in shock as Ant hugged and kissed Shanté. *This nigga been fucking his brother's girl-friend? Is that why he don't want to be a father to our child?* Lashay couldn't believe what she was witnessing and silently prayed that it was all a misunderstanding. However, when she saw them share a passionate kiss, she knew it was no mistake in what she was seeing.

"Girl, what you doing? Is this where you wanna eat at?" Peanut asked as she walked up to Lashay. She stopped talking as soon as she saw the tears coming from her friend's eyes.

"Shay, what the hell wrong with you?" Peanut asked,

confused about what had taken place in the few seconds she'd gone to her car.

"Look inside there and tell me what you see." Lashay pointed, tears still streaming down her face.

Peanut looked into the restaurant where she spotted her cousin, Shanté, and Ant kissing and hugging. Her mouth dropped open in shock as she tried to cover it with her hand. She couldn't believe the same cousin that was fighting her a few months ago for fucking Darius was now fucking Darius' brother.

"Is this why this nigga don't want to be a father to our baby? Because he been fucking her?" Lashay's heart was completely broken, and she couldn't understand why Ant would do something like this to her.

"I say we go in there and ask him what's up. I mean, I know Shanté is my cousin and all, but we ain't been cool since that fight. Like, bitch, how you gon' fight me for fuckin' yo man when you fuckin' his brother?"

Lashay stood there, still looking at the secret couple, with tears in her eyes. "Nah, we ain't going in there. We gonna follow them to wherever they go. I wanna see what the fuck they be doing, so when I go tell Darius, I have all the information," Lashay whispered.

Both Peanut and Lashay walked to Peanut's car where they waited for them to walk out the restaurant. The moment they did, Peanut was on it, starting her car and pulling off right behind them. Lashay shook her head when they pulled up at

Ant's apartment. Lashay watched as Ant got out of his car and walked over to Shanté's car. He opened her door and helped her out of the car before they walked into his building.

"So, what you wanna do now?" Peanut asked.

"We going in."

Peanut followed Lashay as she marched into Ant's apartment building. They walked up to Ant's apartment, and the look on Lashay's face let Peanut know she wasn't there to play any games. The rage on Lashay's face was evident, and Peanut only hoped this wouldn't land them in jail.

Knock, knock, knock!

Lashay banged on Ant's front door like she was the police with a warrant for his arrest. She knew he was home, so there was no way she was leaving until he opened the door. Ant walked over to the front door slowly, hoping it wasn't the police at the door. When he looked out the peephole and saw it was Lashay, he couldn't do anything but shake his head.

"Who's at the door?" Shanté whispered, praying it wasn't Darius.

Before Ant could answer, Lashay began yelling at the top of her lungs.

"Ant, I know you in there, and I know you in there with that bitch. Now, open the fucking door. This what you been doing? Playing the fuck outta me and yo child for yo brother's girlfriend!"

With those words, Ant swung the door open. "Lashay, what the fuck are you doing at my place? And why the fuck are you yelling so loud? I got fucking neighbors. What the fuck do you want?"

"I want to know why the fuck I can't get in contact with you, but I see you out with the next bitch."

"Lashay, I've told you more than once that we are not together. In fact, I been told you that whatever we had was over. You gon' get yo muthafuckin' feelings hurt comin' over here on this shit, dawg."

Shanté just stood there, watching everything that was happening. *Did she just say she was pregnant? Ant told me he wasn't fuckin' with anyone. Now, Lashay, the head hoe of the hood, is standing at his door, saying she pregnant. This nigga got us both pregnant at the same time?* Shanté's eyes widened when she saw Peanut step into view.

"See, this the bullshit right here. You a fuckin' hypocrite. You fightin' me for fuckin' Darius when in real life, you the hoe. Over here fuckin' on his brother. You could have kept lettin' me get that dick cause you clearly been busy ridin' other dicks."

"Look, Lashay, this the last time I'ma tell you and yo home girl to get the fuck outta here. If I gotta say it one more time, shit gon' get ugly!" Ant yelled, clearly fed up with their shenanigans.

With that, Ant attempted to close his door, but Peanut stopped it, placing her foot in the way, so she could say a few more words.

"Shanté, if you think I'm not tellin' Darius what the fuck

y'all got going on, you sadly mistaken. That dick 'bout to be mine again." With that, Peanut walked off, ready to tell Darius everything she knew.

Lashay, still standing there with tears in her eyes, looked up at Ant. "Why don't you want our baby?" she asked quietly.

"Because it's not my baby. I got one baby on the way, and it's the one she carrying," he announced, pointing over at Shanté.

With those words, Lashay had nothing left to say. Her heart felt like it had been broken in two, and she felt like she was about to pass out. Her knees buckled, and she bit her lip to stop the scream that wanted to escape her mouth. She nodded her head slowly before walking away.

"Why did you tell her I was pregnant? Didn't you hear them say they were going to tell Darius we was fuckin'?" Shanté yelled as soon as Ant closed the door.

"What difference does it make if she tells him? You're carrying my baby, so he's gon' find out anyway."

"Yeah, apparently me and Lashay are pregnant by you. But let you tell it, you wasn't fucking with anybody else. So, tell me this. How the fuck is she pregnant by you?"

"I didn't lie to you, Shanté. I ain't fuckin' with nobody but you. I don't even want anyone else but you. Was I fuckin' Lashay? Yes, I was. But I told her we was done with that shit. She knew that before me and you even started seeing each other. It wasn't til weeks later that she even came and told me she was pregnant. I told her to take care of that shit cause I ain't want no ties to that bitch. I only want to be with you, Shanté. That bitch just mad."

Ant walked up and attempted to grab her hands, but Shanté stepped back. Tears filled her eyes as she looked at Ant. She wanted to scream. When Darius cheated on her, it was painful. However, what Ant was doing felt like betrayal. *This nigga saw firsthand how hurt I was by Darius. Then he makes me catch feelings for him, just for him to have me and Lashay pregnant at the same time? Kinda fuck shit is that?* Shanté took deep breaths as she thought before she grabbed her purse and walked out the door without saying another word.

CHAPTER SIX

PRESENT DAY

*A*spen and Brianna sat in the waiting room while Quan and Loke went to go get them a cup of coffee. Their eyes were heavy, and bags had begun to form under them from lack of sleep. It had only been a few hours since they'd gone into surgery. However, to Aspen and Brianna, it felt like an eternity. Loke and Quan stepped back into the waiting room and took their seats next to their girlfriends, handing them both a cup of coffee.

"Did them people hit you up about yo moms yet?" Loke asked.

"Nah, I'm still waiting. Shit, I hope they don't call. At

least until Justice and Tonya get out of surgery. I want to be here when she wakes up," Brianna replied.

"Just know whenever they call, we ridin' out. Fuck all the bullshit. They ain't know y'all had some shooters on y'all team. They gon' know that shit now though," Quan informed.

"Fa' sho'. They bout to see that we don't play no games 'bout y'all," Loke reiterated.

"Thank y'all. I'm glad we can count on y'all," Brianna responded.

"Y'all already know what's up. Next time just don't keep that shit from us. We could have been handled this shit," Loke spoke.

A few moments later, Cream walked into the waiting room. He took a seat across the room without saying a word with worry etched all over his face. He'd never been afraid like this before. The fact that he couldn't control the next phase of his life had him on edge. He'd never prayed before; however, he found himself on his knees several times in the past two days. He needed for God to come through and allow Justice to live because he knew he couldn't live without her.

"You good, bro?" Loke asked, walking over to Cream.

"I will be once my baby out of surgery. I need for her to be good before I'm good," Cream replied.

He hadn't left the hospital since Justice had been shot and didn't plan to do so until she was awake. He wanted his face to be the first one she saw when she woke up. Cream wanted her to know that he'd been by her side the entire time.

"I feel you. Just know we gon' ride out for her. I know it got to be the same people that got Ms. Shanté, so we fo' sho' gon' handle that shit," Loke assured, lowering his tone.

Cream didn't speak, just nodded a thank you. He wanted nothing more than to kill the people that hurt Justice, but he knew he needed to wait. There was no way he was doing anything until Justice was out of surgery and feeling better. So, if Loke and Quan wanted to go in his place, he would let them. *Long as them muthafuckas die, I don't care who the fuck does it.*

Several hours later, Dr. Michaels walked into the waiting room with a serious look on her face. The five of them stood to their feet, ready to hear what the doctor had to say. They all looked at her nervously as they expected the worst.

"Justice's transplant went well. She is out of surgery and doing good. However, we are not out the woods yet. These next seventy-two hours are crucial. This is the time where we ensure that her body accepts the organ and not reject it," she informed.

"What will happen if her body rejects the kidney?" Brianna asked.

"In the event that her body rejects it, we would have to find another donor."

"What will make her body reject it?" Aspen asked.

"The body is designed to fight off foreign things, such as infection and disease. In some cases, the body will see a new organ as a foreign object."

"Do you think that will happen to Justice?" Cream asked.

"We hope not. However, there is no way to tell before-hand. She is being monitored very closely, so in the unfortunate event it does happen, we will be on top of it. I can assure you that we are doing everything we can to make sure Ms. Lewis comes out of this alive."

"When can we see her?" Cream questioned.

"I would like to allow Justice to sleep off the anesthesia. However, once she's awake, you all will be able to go in and see her."

"Thank you for everything, Dr. Michaels. We appreciate you," Cream thanked Dr. Michaels as he shook her hand.

She nodded her head before walking out of the waiting room. "I'm glad she gonna be good," Quan stated.

"The doctor said she might be good. We still don't know yet," Brianna whispered.

"Yeah, I heard what she said. But Justice got her mama's kidney. It's the same blood running through their veins. I think she gonna be good. What the doctor said is just what could happen, not what's gon' happen," Quan continued.

"I hope you right," Cream uttered in a hushed tone.

A few hours later, Dr. Michaels walked back into the waiting room, letting them know that Tonya was awake. She informed them all that if they wanted to see her they could.

"What about Justice?" Cream asked.

"She's still asleep. As soon as she wakes up, I will let you all know."

They followed Dr. Michaels to Tonya's room. She was lying in bed with her eyes closed. However, she opened them as soon as they walked in.

"How you doing, Ms. Tonya?" Cream asked, walking over to her bed.

"I'm okay. How is my baby doing? Did I save her?"

"She's still asleep, so we haven't seen her yet. But Dr. Michaels said that the surgery went well," Cream responded.

Tonya exhaled in relief, happy that Justice's surgery was a success. Knowing that her daughter would be okay was the news she needed to hear. No mother wanted to bury their child, and Tonya was happy she wouldn't have to do so.

"Do you need us to get you anything?" Brianna asked.

"No, I'm fine. The only thing I want now is to see Justice."

Brianna nodded her head, knowing that they all wanted the same thing. Brianna's phone vibrated, letting her know she had a call. Pulling it out of her pocket, she noticed it was the same number that called her the day before. She looked up at Aspen before stepping out of the room.

"Hello?" Brianna answered.

"I hope yo ass got my money." A female spoke into the phone. The voice sounded familiar to Brianna, and she knew she'd heard it before. She just couldn't place it.

"I got yo fuckin' money. You just better hope that my mama ain't hurt. Cause if y'all did anything to her, I swear to God…"

"You swear to God what? Let me tell you something,

bitch. You not in the position to be making threats. That's gon' get you and yo mama fucked up. So, to avoid all that, you gon' shut the fuck up."

Brianna rolled her eyes but didn't say a word. She didn't want to say anything that would upset the caller and make her do something to hurt Shanté. Brianna knew she would have to play their game — at least until she got to the location where her mother was being held.

"Now that we have that out the way, I'm going to text you the address. You and yo little friend are to meet me there at seven tonight. And y'all better come alone. The moment I feel like y'all trying to pull some shit, I'm gon' kill yo mama and make you watch."

Without another word, the phone hung up.

"What did they say?" Aspen whispered as she walked over to Brianna.

"They want us to meet them somewhere at seven. She said we gotta come alone, or they gon' kill my mama."

"We not going alone. Fuck that. You already know Quan and Loke coming with us. We don't know what we walking into, so we gonna need them to have our backs."

"Yeah, you right. They just gon' have to stay out of sight until we need them. I can't risk them doing anything to my mama."

"She gon' be good. We got this, B. Where they want us to meet them at?" Aspen asked.

"I'm not sure. She said she gon' text me the address."

"Okay, cool. Don't worry 'bout shit. I been waiting on this ever since they took her," Aspen informed.

"I hope we got it. I don't know what I would do if anything happened to my mama."

SHANTÉ SAT IN THE BASEMENT AS SHE LOOKED UP AT LASHAY. *Man, I swear when I get myself out of this, I'ma fuck her ass up. I can't believe she did all this shit for some bullshit that happened when we were kids. She should be over that shit by now. Hell, I am. What the fuck is this crazy bitch doing?*

"Don't worry. You gon' find out why you here soon enough," Lashay enlightened, reading the look on Shanté's face.

Like clockwork, Shanté heard the door open and footsteps coming down the stairs. She looked up at Lashay as if to ask her who was coming. Lashay smiled sinisterly, knowing that her plan was working out in her favor. She looked up and watched as her daughter walked down into the basement.

"Shanté, let me introduce you to my daughter, Dominique. Dominique, this is the bitch that is responsible for your father not wanting us."

Dominique walked up to Shanté, looking down on her like she was the dirtiest specimen she'd ever seen. "This is Brianna's mother, right?" she asked.

"Yeah, that's that bitch," Lashay answered.

Without another word, Dominique drew her fist back,

punching Shanté so hard in the face that it tilted the chair she was tied to, causing the chair to fall backwards with Shanté in it.

"Ahhhh!" Shante' screamed before hitting her head hard on the concrete floor.

"That's for my mama!" Dominique yelled. "And this one's for me," she announced , kicking Shanté in her side.

Shanté winced in pain, praying the mother daughter duo wouldn't jump her while she was tied up. "Don't do this," Shante murmured.

"Don't do what? You did this shit to yo'self. I bet you see now that Karma don't have no expiration date," Dominque explained as she stood over Shanté. "Do you know what kind of life I lived because of you? I could have been living good with both my parents in my life. Because of you, I never got to know the love of a father while Brianna had her daddy and mine. My mama told me all the hurt y'all caused her, and now we 'bout to get our revenge for all that shit," she informed, punching Shanté once more in her face.

"Alright, Dominique, don't beat her up too bad. Wait til her daughter gets here so she can watch," Lashay said sinisterly.

Shanté's eyes widened at the mention of her daughter. She didn't want Brianna to be a part of this in any way. *They tryin' to hurt my baby. I ain't 'bout to let that happen. I gotta find a way out of here,* Shanté thought, wanting to do whatever she could to assure Brianna wasn't hurt. Lashay walked over to Dominique, pulling her away from Shanté.

"Send that bitch the address so we can get this shit over with. Pretty soon, we gon' have all these bitches right where we want them," Lashay suggested.

"Please, my daughter don't have anything to do with this. We can keep this between us. Ain't no need to involve Brianna."

"That bitch got everything to do with this. You ruined my mama life, and yo daughter and her friends ruined mine. All y'all bitches gon' get what y'all deserve today," Dominique informed.

Shanté was confused by what was happening. As far as she knew, this didn't involve anyone else except her and Lashay. *Brianna and her friends don't have shit to do with this. Why the hell do they keep mentioning them?* Shanté watched as Dominique reached into her purse and pulled out her cellphone. She then shot Brianna a quick text, giving her an address and a time to meet them, giving her only an hour to get there.

CHAPTER SEVEN

"Y'all gon' have to handle that shit without me. My baby just got out of surgery. Ain't no way I'm leaving her side right now. Just make sure y'all get them muthafuckas that did this shit," Cream spoke once Brianna let them all know what was going on.

"You know we got you. Whoever did this shit ain't gon' be breathin' tomorrow. I can promise you that shit," Loke explained.

"Fa sho. We not letting up on they asses," Quan stated.

"That's what I like to hear. Fuck them niggas up," Cream reiterated. "And y'all be careful." He stood there watching as they all walked out the room on their way to handle business. Cream took his seat next to Justice's bedside. Although she had woken up after surgery, she was still in and out of sleep due to the medication they had going through her IV.

"I'm so happy you're okay, baby. I wouldn't know what to do without you," Cream whispered in Justice's ear before kissing her on her forehead.

A few moments later, Tonya was being wheeled into the room. "I told her she should be resting after surgery, but she wouldn't take no for an answer. She was determined to see her daughter, so I had to bring her," the nurse stated, locking Tonya's wheelchair on the opposite side of Justice's bed.

Cream nodded his head, already knowing Tonya was coming to see Justice as soon as she woke up.

"I thought she'd woken up from surgery?" Tonya inquired.

"She has. She's just still a bit drowsy from the medication," the nurse informed. "I'll be back a little bit later to take you back to your room. You have to get your rest as well. I know you want to be here for your daughter, but you just had major surgery too. And you need to allow your body to heal."

Tonya nodded as she watched the nurse walk out of the room. Tears of joy fell from her eyes as she looked over at her daughter. She was proud that she could be the one to save her life.

"I'm so glad you gonna be okay, baby," Tonya whispered.

"Me too," Creamed agreed. The two of them sat by Justice's bedside until the nurse came to get Tonya to take her back to her room.

. . .

"We need to get strapped up. Ain't no telling what we 'bout to walk into," Quan suggested.

"I'm already on it. Follow us back to the house. I got everything we gon' need at the crib," Loke informed.

Quan nodded his head and got in the car with Aspen before they all pulled off, following Loke and Brianna to their house. When they pulled into their driveway, they all jumped out of their cars and went into the house. Loke motioned for Quan to follow him as he led him into the basement. Loke walked over to a bookcase in the far corner and opened the bottom drawer, revealing the location of all his firearms. Loke began retrieving guns from the purple velvet lined drawer and loading them. When he was done, he handed two pistols to Quan.

"Damn, you think we gon' need all these?" Quan asked, looking down at the guns.

"It's better to be safe than sorry. I don't know what all we gon' need, but we gon' have it wit' us."

Quan nodded his head, agreeing with Loke. "I see you ready to fuck some shit up, huh?"

"Hell yeah. They got away with this shit for way too long. It's time for us to step in and show them who they niggas really are," Loke boasted, holding one of his guns in the air. "I'm ready for all the shits."

"I see that. Don't you think you a bit too eager to do this shit? Fuck we gettin' into for real? What if this shit backfires on us?" Quan asked.

"Nigga, I know you ain't runnin' scared now? We in this shit, and we ain't got no choice but to handle business. Now, if you having second thoughts, let me know now, and I'll ride out myself," Loke spoke out in irritation.

"Nigga, you know I'm down for whatever. I was just sayin'."

"What was you sayin'? Cause from what I heard, it sounded like second thoughts to me," Loke asked, walking up closely to Quan.

"I'm just sayin' calm down and stay alert. It's not just us we gotta look out for."

"Don't you think I know that, nigga? I'm doing this shit for them. When they fucked with them, they fucked with me. So, this is revenge for us all," Loke announced.

Quan nodded his head, placing the guns in his waistband.

ASPEN SAT ON BRIANNA'S BED AS SHE WATCHED HER TAKE guns from her nightstand drawer. She watched in silence as Brianna went to her closet and retrieved a box of bullets. Brianna had begun loading the guns when she heard Aspen whisper something under her breath.

"What you say? I didn't hear you," Brianna asked.

"I said I'm pregnant," she whispered.

Brianna placed the gun on the nightstand and took a seat on the bed next to Aspen. "When the hell did you find this out?"

"Today at the hospital. That's the reason why I couldn't have the surgery to give Justice my kidney."

"Does Quan know yet?"

"Hell nah. If he knew, I wouldn't be able to go with you to go get Ms. Shanté."

"Well, if you would have been the one to give Justice the kidney, then you wouldn't be going anyway. So, what's the difference?"

"You right, but I didn't give the kidney. And I think that was a sign."

"A sign for what? What you mean?" Brianna asked.

"I don't know. I just feel like I'm supposed to be there. What if something goes wrong, and I need to help? I would just feel much better being there with you. Once all this is over, then I'll tell Quan," Aspen assured.

"You just make sure you be extra careful. You got my niece or nephew inside there," Brianna said, rubbing Aspen's stomach. "I can't believe I'm about to be an auntie," she cooed.

"Girl, I can't believe I'm about to be a mother."

"Let's go get my mama, so we can get back and plan this gender reveal."

Brianna finished loading the guns before handing two of them to Aspen. She placed one in her purse and the other in an ankle holster. She also placed a small knife in her back pocket, not knowing what all she would need.

"You ready?" Aspen asked, looking over at Brianna.

"I stay ready. Just let me shoot this text to Cream. I wanna give him the address, just in case something happens. Then we can head out."

Once the text was sent, both Aspen and Brianna walked down the stairs. They noticed that Loke and Quan were already in the living room, ready to go. "Y'all good?" Quan asked.

"Yeah, we good. Y'all ready to ride out?" Aspen asked.

"Hell yeah, sis. You already know what it is," Loke confirmed.

The four of them walked out the door, all piling into Aspen's car, before she pulled off, heading to the address where Shanté was being held.

CHAPTER EIGHT

ominque took a seat directly in front of where Shanté sat. After sending the text to Brianna, telling them where they were, there was nothing left to do but wait. She was eager to see the look on their faces when they found out they were all about to die anyway. *I'll take they money, but none of these bitches gonna leave this house alive no matter what.* Dominique smiled at her sinister thoughts before chuckling a bit. Dominique was in full on revenge mode and couldn't wait to get active.

"Please don't do this. Whatever beef me and yo mama had is twenty years old. Ant is dead, so I really don't understand why all this is happening now. Please just let me go," Shanté pleaded.

"You ain't going nowhere. This ain't about you and my momma for me. I got my own beef," Dominique declared.

"What do you mean?" Shanté inquired.

"You will see soon enough."

CREAM SAT IN A CHAIR NEXT TO JUSTICE'S BEDSIDE AS HE scrolled TikTok. He was extremely tired and wanted a hot shower. However, he refused to leave Justice's side.

"Baby, what happened?" Justice spoke weakly. Her throat was so dry that it hurt. She tried to swallow her own saliva in an effort to moisten her mouth, but it was to no avail.

"Justice, baby. Oh, my God. I'm so happy you're awake. I thought I was gon' lose you. You got shot, Jay," he reported.

"I feel like I just got hit by a mack truck."

"I bet. You had to get two surgeries. One was a kidney transplant."

"Where's my mama?" Justice asked, looking around the room and seeing nobody but Cream.

"She's here. She's in a room upstairs. She had surgery to give you her kidney," Cream informed.

"Damn, my mama always have my back. Where is Aspen and Brianna?"

"They had to go handle some business, but they will be back later. Baby, I have to ask you something real important. What do you remember about what happened?" Cream questioned.

"Where did they go? Did they tell you what they were going to do?" Justice asked frantically. She tried to sit up in bed, but the pain got the best of her, causing her to fall back on her pillow.

"Baby, relax, don't move. You just had major surgery. The last thing you want to do is bust yo stitches."

"Cream, did they tell you where they were going?" Justice asked again.

"They actually told me everything. I know y'all been hittin' licks on these niggas out here," he answered.

Justice dropped her head shamefully. She never wanted Cream to find out what she did for a living, and she damn sure didn't want him to find out from someone else's mouth. However, it was too late for all that now. The worst had happened, and she knew her girls had no choice but to tell him.

"So, you know about all that, huh?"

"Yeah, they told me everything. I know about Ms. Shanté being kidnapped too. That's the business they had to go handle. They going to get her back," Cream informed.

"They went by themselves? Cream, why didn't you go with them?"

"Jay, are you crazy? I wasn't going nowhere til I knew you were good. And they ain't go alone. Quan and Loke went with them."

With those words, Justice's eyes widened. "Oh, my God! Where is my phone? I need to call them. I have to warn them. Cream, please give me my phone." Justice was beyond frantic now, and Cream didn't understand why.

Maybe it's the medicine she coming off of that got her acting like that, he thought.

"Baby, calm down. You didn't hear me say Quan and Loke went with them? They good. Them niggas ain't gon' let nothing happen to them."

"Cream, you don't understand. Loke is the one who shot our truck up. They in danger."

SEVERAL MOMENTS LATER, ASPEN, BRIANNA, QUAN, AND Loke pulled up to the address that was sent to Brianna. Much to their surprise, they were in front of a house. They looked at the address, confused.

"This where they got her?" Aspen asked.

"I guess so. This the address they sent me."

"Hit them up and tell them we outside," Quan suggested.

Agreeing with Quan, Brianna grabbed her phone and shot a text to the number that had been contacting her. When the number texted back, telling her to come inside, she got out the car with the others following her. The four of them walked onto the porch slowly, looking around to make sure nobody was watching them. Quan pulled his gun from his waistline and motioned for Brianna to knock on the door. When she did, the door opened, and Quan walked inside first. Gun raised, he walked through the front of the house, making sure to pay close attention to his surroundings. Aspen and Brianna were both close behind him with their guns out too, while Loke was behind them.

"Where they at? It don't look like nobody's even here." Quan noticed.

"They got to be here. This is the address they gave me," Brianna whispered.

"Call them muthafuckas and see what's up. I ain't got time for them to be playing games," Loke suggested.

As if on cue, Lashay walked down the steps, gun in hand. She pointed the gun at Brianna and then at Aspen, telling them both to lower their weapons. She walked up on them slowly and asked them for the money she'd requested.

"Don't I know you? Yeah, you was that bitch at my uncle's funeral. You fucked up my whole life that day." Brianna remembered.

"You mean yo daddy's funeral. And I ain't fuck yo life up. You mama did that all on her own. But you seem like you been doing a good job of fuckin' the rest up yo'self."

Before Brianna could say another word, she was hit in the head so hard that she went crashing to the floor.

"What the fuck?" Aspen yelled out once she heard Brianna hit the floor. She raised her gun, but before she could shoot, she was sent crashing to the floor right next to Brianna.

"Maliki, you and Quan take these bitches down in the basement. Yo sister down there already. She can show y'all where to put these hoes," Lashay ordered.

"Okay, Mama, I got you," Loke responded, picking

Brianna up and throwing her over his shoulder. Quan did the same, and they took both girls down to the basement where Dominique was waiting.

"What up doe, y'all?" Dominique greeted both her brother and her cousin happily as she watched them bring in the two people she'd been waiting for.

"Noooooo, not my babies! Please tell me you didn't hurt them," Shanté cried, noticing they were bringing both Aspen and Brianna down unconscious.

"Bitch, shut the fuck up!" Dominque yelled, rushing over to Shanté, punching her dead in the mouth and busting her lip.

"Where you want us to put them?" Quan asked, referring to Aspen and Brianna.

"Tie them to them pipes over there in the corner." Dominique pointed.

"Please just let them go. You can do whatever you want to me, but they don't have shit to do with this," Shanté pleaded. "Loke, Quan, what are y'all doing? Y'all were supposed to love them," she continued.

"Love? I don't love no bitch but my mama. Them hoes was all part of the plan to get y'all where y'all are now. We had to show y'all that y'all fucked with the wrong family," Loke responded.

Shanté was in disbelief as she heard the words that exited his mouth. She knew how much both Brianna and Aspen loved their boyfriends, so finding out that this was all a setup would crush them. Shanté just didn't understand why any of this was going on, and she needed for someone to tell her something quickly.

CREAM'S EYES WIDENED AT THE NEWS AS HE RAN HIS HAND over his head. This was all becoming too much for him, and he didn't understand what was going on. *I know I didn't just hear what I think I heard. Ain't no fuckin' way. That nigga been here at the hospital praying that Justice made it out alive. Said he wanted to ride out for her and everything. How could he be the one that pulled the trigger?* Cream thought.

"What do you mean Loke was the one that shot you?" Cream asked, hoping that wasn't what Justice had said.

"Loke shot me, babe. I saw him aim the gun out the window and point it at the car. Before I could do anything, he started blastin'. But baby, I know it was him. That nigga ain't have nothing coverin' his face, so I saw that shit clear as day. You gotta go find them, baby. I can't lose my best friend or my cousin."

"Fuck!" Cream shouted, a little louder than he intended.

He thought for a moment before he remembered that Brianna had sent him the address. As much as he didn't want to leave Justice at the hospital, he knew she would never forgive him if anything happened to Aspen or Brianna.

"I know where they at. Bri sent me the addy. I'll go over there and see what's up," Cream reasoned.

"Okay, but don't go alone. You don't know who or what is over there. Take Joc with you or somethin'."

"Okay, I got you, baby," Cream responded, kissing Justice on her forehead.

"Be safe, baby."

"I got you, boo. I'ma go get Aspen and Brianna and bring them back here. I know they gonna be happy that you up and talking."

Justice watched as Cream walked out of her hospital room door. She was terrified for her friends, knowing Loke would do anything to hurt them. *He tried to kill us, but why?* Justice didn't understand what was going on, and the thought of it all made her head hurt. She knew she wasn't wrong about Loke being the one that shot her. It was the why that had her mind spinning.

CREAM SAT IN HIS CAR IN THE PARKING LOT OF THE HOSPITAL and called his cousin. He was angry and ready to cause some damage. Loke was supposed to be family. As her cousin's man, he would have been the last person he would have thought shot Justice, but there they were.

"What up doe?" Joc answered.

"Yo, I need you to ride out with me. Some shit done went down, and I might need yo help," Cream informed.

"Fa sho, you know I got you. I'm at the crib."

"Cool, I'm on my way. Thanks, cuz."

Cream wasted no time making his way to Joc's house. He was in a rage as he floated down Outer Drive. *This nigga smiled in my face. All the while, he was the one that shot Justice. Fuck is he on?*

When Cream pulled up to Joc's house, there was no need to go inside. Joc was waiting for him on the porch with a duffle bag over his shoulder. "See, this why this nigga is my favorite cousin. This nigga always down to ride," Cream said aloud to himself.

Joc put the duffle bag in the backseat before getting in the front. "I ain't know what was up, so I brought us some extra heat," Joc informed, pointing to the bag.

"Good, cause we probably gon' need it."

"Aww, shit, tell a nigga what happened."

Cream pulled off before he responded. "Justice got shot yesterday. When she woke up today, she remembered everything."

"Oh, so she knows who shot her? Yeah, we gon' get that muthafucka. Who the fuck did that hoe ass shit?" Joc asked.

"Loke."

"You talkin' bout her homegirl's nigga? Why the fuck would he shoot Justice?"

"That's what I wanna know. He shot the whole car up. All three of them were in it, but Justice was the one hit. Aspen and Brianna with him now. Justice sent me to go get them. But you already know I'm 'bout to kill that nigga," Cream replied.

"Hell yeah, it's over for his ass. How is Justice?"

"She'd just woke up from the surgery she had right before I left. She had to have a kidney transplant. I didn't want to leave her. But I knew she would never forgive me if I didn't at least try to save her girls. The crazy part is that nigga was all up at the hospital, actin' sad and shit. Nigga gon' tell me that we was gon' ride out for Justice. All the while, his ass was the one that pulled the trigger."

"Damn, he a snake ass nigga," Joc observed.

"Shit, he a dead ass nigga."

Cream did ninety down the Southfield Freeway, wanting to get to the address as fast as he could. His trigger finger itched the closer he got to the house, and he was ready for whatever came to him. Loke had tried to kill Justice, so for that, he had to die. When Cream pulled up to the house, he grabbed the duffle bag from the backseat, and both him and Joc began pulling out guns.

ASPEN STARTED TO WAKE UP. HER HEAD WAS POUNDING, AND she had no clue what had happened. She tried to touch the back of her head in an attempt to ease the pain but couldn't move her arms. She looked down to find she was tied up. *What the fuck?* She looked around frantically and saw Brianna tied to a pipe next to her, unconscious. When she looked over to her left, she saw Loke and Quan talking to someone she couldn't see. She could also see Ms. Shanté tied to a chair next to them. She seemed to be crying, and Aspen called out to her, letting her know everything would be okay.

"Baby, help me. Come untie me," Aspen called out to Quan.

However, he didn't say a word. Loke stepped to the side, allowing Aspen to see who he and Quan were talking to. When she looked into the eyes of Dominique, she was dumbfounded. *What the fuck is she doing here?* Dominique, seeing that Aspen was awake, started walking over to her.

"Yeah, bitch, I see you up now. I been waiting for this moment," Dominique announced sinisterly. When she looked over at Brianna and saw she still wasn't awake, she slapped her in the face, trying to wake her quicker. She was tired of waiting and was ready to get this shit started. Dominique felt she had waited long enough and wasn't about to wait another second.

"Get the fuck up, bitch!" she yelled.

Aspen looked over to Loke and Quan for help. However, when Loke walked over to Brianna and forced her awake, she knew no help was coming from them.

"What the fuck is going on?" Aspen asked, looking up at Quan. "Why are you just standing there? Loke, what the fuck are you doing? Help us!"

"Oh, bitch, you gon' sit there and act like you don't know why you here? Come on, Aspen, don't do that shit. You already know what's up," Loke stated.

Just then, Lashay stepped into view. "Well, now that you're all here and awake, let the show begin. See, I was once in love with a man, your father," Lashay spoke, looking over at Brianna, who was now awake and just as shocked as Aspen.

"But that man didn't love me. In fact, he broke my heart over some bitch that didn't even love him. I could have given him a good life with as many children as he wanted. But instead, he chose some bitch that didn't even want to tell anyone he was the father of her child. That bitch ruined my life. And for years, I let it slid. Imagine my surprise when I found out that my enemy now had a daughter, a niece, and a friend that was fuckin' up my children's lives," she continued, looking from Shanté to Brianna and Aspen.

"What the fuck are you talking about? We don't even know you. I know Dominique from school, but we don't know each other like that. We ain't never did shit to y'all!" Brianna yelled out, confused. She didn't understand how her and Aspen were tied up while Loke and Quan just stood there.

"See, that's where the fuck you're wrong. Dominique is your sister, and maybe if you would have known that, none of this would have happened. I put that shit on yo mama too. That's her fault the two of you didn't know each other. Y'all wanna know something? It's every mother's worst fear to have to bury their child. No mother should have to go through that. But because of y'all, I know what that feels like firsthand. Y'all killed my baby, and the day I found out he died was the day I vowed to avenge his death. So, now your mother will feel the same pain I did."

"Girl, you are fuckin' sick. My girls didn't kill anyone. You got us down here for some made up story? You need mental help, and you bet not touch neither one of them. Girl, I swear if I wasn't tied the fuck up," Shanté challenged. She knew her daughter. Shanté had raised both Brianna and Aspen, so she knew neither of them could be capable of murder. Lashay was all over the place, and Shanté couldn't help but think she was going crazy.

"If you wasn't tied up, you still wouldn't do shit," Lashay shot back.

Lashay had waited long enough to finally have her son's murders in reach. Now that she had them, she was going to assure they felt every ounce of pain she'd felt. Her son was gone, and he wasn't coming back. In her eyes, Shanté needed to suffer the same way she had.

"We don't even know who your son is, so there's no way we killed him," Aspen spoke up.

"Now, what you not gon' do is play in my face. Bitch, we know it was y'all. Y'all was robbin' all them dope spots cause y'all hood rat asses couldn't get money of y'all own. Y'all shot my baby as he was walking into the house. Then y'all left him there to die like he was trash."

Aspen thought back to the lick they hit on Grill's spot where they had caught their first two bodies. *Oh, my God, one of them dudes was her son.* Lashay noticed the look on Aspen's face and knew that she knew exactly what she was referring to.

"Yeah, bitch, I see you got yo memory back now! Oh, but y'all couldn't stop there. Y'all had to keep on killin' my people, huh?"

Brianna looked over at her mother in shame. Here she was, tied to a pipe and possibly about to lose her life. However, all she could think about was the fact that her mother was hearing all about a life that Brianna tried to keep from her. Her deepest secrets were being laid out on a platter for her mother to hear, and Brianna was ashamed.

"Killin' my brother wasn't enough for y'all. Y'all had to kill my man too. Aspen, you a bitter ass bitch that need to be on an episode of *Fatal Attraction*. Killin' a nigga cause he don't want you. Bitch, if you thought I wasn't gon' get at you 'bout my nigga, you sadly mistaken." Dominique chimed in.

She walked up to Aspen and kicked her in the face, sending blood and spittle flying from her mouth. Shanté screamed, trying her best to untie herself. All she could think about was saving Brianna and Aspen. There was so much being said, and Shanté didn't know if it was all true. She just knew she couldn't allow them to hurt Brianna or Aspen.

Aspen looked over at Quan, hurt evident in her face. All she could do was shake her head. Quan stood there, looking down at her with cold eyes.

"Aspen was not bitter. She didn't even want Moe anymore. He wouldn't even be dead if he would have never busted up in Aspen's house that night on bullshit. He tried to rape her," Brianna revealed. "Loke, what are you doing? I thought you loved me. You just gon' stand there and watch all this shit go down? Fuck is going on?" Brianna asked, looking up at Loke with tears in her eyes. Her mouth trembled as she spoke, and her eyes pleaded with him.

"Sorry, baby, that's just how the cookie crumbles," Loke stated coldly.

"Bitch, you even dumber than you look. You killed his brother and his sister's boyfriend, and you think he really loved you? Bitch, all this was a setup to lead up to this very day," Lashay revealed.

She lit a cigarette and took a seat on the basement stairs. She took a long drag of the Newport and exhaled before she spoke again, recounting the events that led them there.

"After y'all killed my son, we didn't know who did it. It wasn't until Moe went to Dominique and told her he thought y'all were the ones that robbed him and the other dope spots. That's when y'all got on my radar. I put a few people on y'all, and we saw y'all hittin' different spots, so we knew."

Lashay's eyes were cold with no remorse in them. Shanté knew that if she didn't untie herself quickly, they would hurt both Brianna and Aspen. Her heart pounded as she began working on getting her hands loose.

"The night Moe went over there, I tried to go with him.

But he told me he didn't want anything to happen to me. When he didn't come back that night, I already knew he was gone, but I tried to hold out hope. But I knew my man. There was no way he wouldn't come home to our family unless something happened to him. Imagine having to raise a child and that child never being able to know how great her daddy was." Dominique chimed in.

"We been putting together this plan since then. But the award goes to Loke and Quan. Y'all bitches actually believed they loved y'all. Damn, Shanté, you ain't teach these girls shit," Lashay announced. "Loke was down for it, and he originally was gonna fuck with Aspen, but since Quan was gonna get the other one, we couldn't do that. I couldn't have Brianna fucking her own cousin. That would have been too much, even for me. It would have really fucked her up though, don't you think?" Lashay laughed.

Shanté looked over at her in disbelief. *Now I now this bitch has lost her mind. Quan is not Brianna's damn cousin. This bitch is fuckin' crazy,* she thought to herself.

"Girl, why are you lying? Quan is not her cousin," Shanté shouted. "Tell the fuckin' story without yo lying ass theatrics. Now I let you come in and tell my daughter who her real father was. And if they wouldn't have pulled me off of you, they would have been burying yo ass with Ant. But what you not 'bout to do is just be addin' in family members. You are one sick ass bitch."

"Right, Quan is Loke's cousin. We all know that." Brianna

chimed in. All she wanted was for this to be over with. She was hurt about Loke not really being down for her. As much love as she'd shown him throughout their entire relationship, he'd played her in the end. At that moment, Brianna didn't care what happened to her. She just wanted them to get to it.

"You right. Quan is Loke's cousin. That wasn't a lie. But that is only because his mother is my best friend. Quan, baby, tell them who yo mama is," Lashay coached.

"My mama's name is Tamika, but the family calls her Peanut," Quan revealed.

"I don't know no damn Peanut!" Brianna yelled.

"Peanut is my cousin on my daddy's side. We stopped talking years ago when I was a teen. She did a lot of crazy stuff to me and wasn't a good cousin. I haven't talked to her since then. You already know I don't talk to my daddy's side of the family anyway. She was like the only one that I really talked to — until I didn't," Shanté recalled.

"So, Quan is really my fuckin' cousin?" Brianna asked. Brianna couldn't do anything but shake her head. For the second time within a month, she was finding out who her real family members were, and she wasn't liking that shit.

"If Peanut is his mama, then yeah. I've never met any of her kids. Hell, I didn't even know she had any," Shanté responded, not believing what was unfolding right in front of her eyes. This had all been one big plan to take them all down. She just didn't understand how, after all this time, their families were still crossing paths.

"You really don't love me, Quan? Like for real, how could you have been in on all this shit? How could this all have been a lie? I thought we were in love, and you never cared?" Aspen asked, looking up into his eyes. *How could everything have been fake?* Her heart was crushed, and she couldn't understand why he would do something so cruel. Quan didn't say a word, only looked at Aspen, and she nodded her head, already knowing the answer.

"What do y'all want with us? I know y'all didn't bring us here just to let us know y'all been fucking up our lives for over a year. I'm sick of all this talkin' shit. Let's get active," Brianna challenged, sick of the back-and-forth. She knew they wanted to kill them, and she just wanted them to get it over with. The pain in her chest was so great that she felt dying would hurt less.

"Bitch, you not gonna rush me! All this time and planning I put into this. Bitch, you gon' hear every word!" Lashay yelled. "So, after Loke and Quan agreed to go in undercover, for a lack of a better phrase, we started following y'all. We knew y'all every move without y'all even knowing. Y'all remember that Kalamazoo hit, right?" Lashay asked, looking over at both Aspen and Brianna.

Brianna didn't need to hear anymore. She knew exactly what Lashay was about to say. Anger shot through her entire body. All she saw was red as her hurt quickly turned to rage. She wanted to murder Lashay with her bare hands. "You killed Ant?" Brianna yelled as she tired her best to untie herself.

"You finally smartening up, little girl. That nigga had to go for what he did to me and my child. Telling you he was your real father at his funeral was just a bonus, a little extra added hurt. That was Dominique's idea. and now, since y'all know everything, I can finally feel the joy of killing you all," Lashay revealed as she pulled out a gun.

CHAPTER NINE

Joc picked the lock on the door and opened it slowly. They both walked in, guns aimed and ready to shoot. They walked through the house, looking for Aspen and Brianna. "I hear voices coming from down here," Joc whispered, pointing at the door that led to the basement. Cream nodded and walked toward the door. He could hear the voices too, and he knew one of them was Brianna's but didn't know who the other one belonged to. He heard Brianna yell out that she was going to kill someone. Before they could open the door all the way, they heard two gunshots. Cream and Joc ran down the steps, guns ready to shoot.

When they got into the basement, the first thing they saw was Ms. Shanté trying to wrestle a gun out the hands of some woman. From there, Cream saw Loke. Without one word, he shot twice, hitting Loke in the head, causing him to fall to the floor.

"Noooo, Maliki. Please no!" Lashay yelled out, breaking her tussle with Shanté and running over to her son. She cradled his body in her hands as she cried. Dominique stood there in shock, not knowing how things had taken a turn for the worst so quickly. Not knowing what type of time Quan was on, Joc sent two to his stomach before watching him fall. Lashay screamed again, looking over at Quan lying on the floor.

Dominique, thinking quick on her feet, pulled her gun and fired shots in Joc's direction. However, she was such a bad shot that every shot she fired missed, giving Joc open space to shoot her. Lashay was done for when she saw her baby girl hit the floor. Before anyone knew what was happening, Lashay ran over to Joc and punched him so hard in the face that it made him drop his gun. She bent down to pick it up, but before she could, Shanté shot her three times in the back, putting her down permanently and causing all of their troubles to go away.

"Are y'all okay?" Cream asked, rushing over to the both of them.

He untied Aspen as Shanté untied Brianna. "Cream, how did you know what was going on?" Aspen asked.

"Justice woke up after surgery and told me that she saw the shooter, and it was Loke."

"What surgery? Justice was shot?" Shanté asked frantically, not knowing any of that had happened.

"Yes, but she's okay now. She had to get a kidney transplant. Ms. Tonya gave her one of her kidneys," Cream informed.

"Oh, my God. I'm gonna have to go see her," Shanté replied.

"You can go see her tomorrow, Ma. Tonight, you need to rest." Brianna chimed in. Shanté nodded her head, knowing Brianna was right. The last few days had been a lot for her. She needed a hot bath, a meal, and her own bed.

"Come on. Let me take y'all home," Cream suggested. "Aspen, you good?" he asked, noticing Aspen in a trance looking down at Quan's body. Although she'd just found out the evil truth about him, her feelings were still there. The fact that he was lying dead right in front of her crushed her. She had his child growing inside of her, and he was no longer. *If he would have known I was pregnant, would that have of changed anything?* Aspen asked herself, knowing she would never know the answer to that question.

"Yeah, I'm okay. Ms. Shanté, can I spend the night at yo house tonight? I really don't want to be alone."

"Of course you can, baby. You both can. I would much rather have y'all with me tonight."

"I was already comin'," Brianna spoke up.

Shanté smiled and hugged both Brianna and Aspen before

they all walked to Cream's car, heading back to Shanté's house.

CHAPTER TEN

"Damn, I forgot how this house looked. I can't do nothing until after I clean it up," Shanté stated, walking into her home for the first time in days.

"Don't worry, Mama. We gon' help you, and I'll order us some food off of Door Dash."

"Yeah, it won't take long for us to clean if all three of us doing it," Aspen suggested.

The three of them got to work, cleaning up every inch of the house, and by the time their food got there, everything was clean. They all piled their plates with Chinese food and took a seat at Shanté's dining room table. They silently ate, not having any type of conversation. Nothing was on their minds except the events that had just taken place.

When they were done eating, Aspen went into one of the upstairs bathrooms to take a shower. She was more than exhausted, and all she wanted was a shower and a bed. The fact that she was going to be sleeping alone for the first time in over a year made Aspen sad. Knowing Quan wasn't coming back made her even sadder. She'd heard all the words Lashay had said. She'd also saw everything that had taken place. Yet it still felt unbelievable that Quan's love for her was fake. *What type of person would do that? I thought I was gonna marry that man.*

Aspen got into the shower and let the hot water run down her body. She washed herself several times in an effort to wash the hurt away. She wished she could pull her heart from her chest and run it underneath the water as well. Maybe then she would be able to wash away the pain of betrayal, the agony of his lies, and the suffering of knowing she was still carrying his child. She just wished it could all mix with the water and go down the drain. However, that wasn't reality. Honestly, nothing but time could make the feeling go away, and Aspen didn't know if she could take it.

"He didn't have to take it this far. Why would he be the one to hurt me? I fucking loved him with all my heart. Now he's dead and can't even explain himself," Aspen cried, sliding down the shower wall, allowing the hot water to run down her face and mix with her tears.

Once she finally got out of the shower, she wrapped a towel around her wet body and walked into the guest bedroom. Going into one of the drawers, she pulled out one of the cotton nightgowns that was neatly folded inside. She slid it over her head before crawling into the bed and getting underneath the covers.

"How you feeling, baby? Are you holding up okay?" Shanté asked, walking into Brianna's old room.

"No, but I guess I don't have a choice but to be okay."

Shanté walked over and sat on the bed next to Brianna. She knew all too well about being hurt by someone that was supposed to love you, and she hated her daughter was going through that.

"I thought he was good for me. I truly loved him. I thought that this time I had found the person that was going to save me," Brianna whispered, silent tears streaming from her eyes.

Shanté pulled her daughter closer. "I know what you mean. I thought Ant was going to save me too. He probably would have, but I didn't give him a real chance."

"Ma, did you love Ant?"

"I loved him very much. Ant was the love of my life," Shanté answered truthfully.

"What happened with that? I want to hear the story."

December 2004

It was a few weeks before Christmas, and Shanté was at the mall doing some last-minute shopping. It had been weeks since she'd spoken to Ant, and she hated it. She wanted to call him and tell him how much she missed him, but she felt too played. The fact that Ant knew how hurt she was by Darius made what he did ten times worse. He hadn't so much as called her since the day she stormed out of his apartment.

Shanté walked out the mall, bags in hand as she headed to her car. She had been shopping all day, and all she wanted was to curl up in her bed and watch a movie. She pulled up to her house to see Darius was parked in front of it. He got out his car when he saw her pull up. He was eager to speak with her. Darius had heard around the hood that Shanté was pregnant, and he wanted to hear it from her.

"Where you coming from?" Darius asked, opening Shanté's car door and allowing her to step out.

"Northland. I had some Christmas shopping to do," she replied, popping her trunk and grabbing her shopping bags.

"Let me get those for you," Darius offered, taking the bags from Shanté's hands.

"Thank you," she replied.

Shanté and Darius had been on speaking terms for the past two weeks. Although they were not back together, she did feel that he was truly sorry. So, she decided to let him back in little by little. She didn't know if it was because she missed him or the fact that she was pregnant by his brother; but Shanté decided to forgive him.

"You can just sit the bags on the couch," Shanté informed, walking into the kitchen and grabbing two bottles of water.

She handed one to Darius before taking a seat on the opposite end of the couch. "So, what brings you by?" she asked.

Darius looked deep into her eyes and over her body. He wanted to know if there was any change in her appearance that would tell him she was pregnant without him asking. Other than her cheeks being a bit more puffy than normal, there was nothing else. So, he decided to just come out and ask.

"Shanté, I been hearing some stuff around the hood, and I just wanted to ask you straight up."

Shanté looked at him with wide eyes. *Lord, please don't let this man ask me anything about his brother,* she thought to herself. "What did you hear?" she asked skeptically.

"Shanté, are you pregnant? I mean, that's what the streets been saying, and I'm just trying to find out if it's true."

Shanté dropped her head low, but it was not in shame for the baby she was carrying. Her shame was in the fact that Darius had to find out from other people. One thing Shanté would say was that no matter how many times Darius cheated, he had never brought a baby back home.

"Yes, Darius. It's true. I'm pregnant."

"How far along are you?" he asked.

"I'm three months. Look, I'm sorry that you had…" Before Shanté could even finish her sentence, Darius rushed over to her, wrapping his arms around her and pulling her into his embrace.

"Baby, this ain't nothing but God. I prayed every night for him to show you that we are supposed to be together. These last few months that we've been apart has been hell on me. Now look at God! Like my mama always says, 'won't he do it!' You being pregnant with my child is the sign we both needed that this was meant to be. I'm about to be a father!" Darius cheered.

"Darius, I don't think you…"

"It's okay." Darius cut her off again. "I know we have a lot to work on before we get back to how we were. And I'm willing to put in as much work as I need to. We are about to be a family, baby. And I promise you that I will never let anyone or anything come between that."

Tears filled Shanté's eyes, and Darius wiped each one away as they fell down her cheeks. Shanté had waited years for Darius to tell her he was ready to take their relationship seriously. He was telling her everything she dreamed of hearing since they'd first gotten together over two years ago. However, his timing was all wrong. Shanté was sitting there, pregnant by his brother, and Darius thought the baby was his.

"Darius, this… this baby don't…" Shanté tried to speak, but Darius cut her off once more.

"I know this baby don't mean we just gon' jump right back into things. Like I said, I'm willing to put in the work. I'm going to take care of my family, and we gon' be good. I promise you and our child won't want for anything mentally, physically, or emotionally. Today, Darius the boy is no longer. I will now and forever be Darius the man," he announced.

"You want something to eat? I can go down to the Coney and get you something."

"Yeah, let me get a ten-piece, fried hard, all flats, and some chili cheese fries. But you know I only fuck with squeeze. None of that sliced shit on mine," Shanté informed, referring to the type of cheese she wanted on her fries.

"Whattttt? So, you don't want a corned beef on an onion roll?" Darius asked, already knowing her usual order.

"Nah, this baby got me eating different. I don't think this baby likes anything but chicken and Caeser salads." They both laughed, and Darius walked out the house, heading to the restaurant.

"Fuck, what the fuck am I gon' do? This nigga thinks the baby is his. How the fuck am I supposed to tell him that my baby belongs to Ant?" Shanté said aloud to herself. She didn't know what she was going to say or how she was going to say it, but she knew she had to. There was no way she could allow Darius to think he was the father of another man's baby. However, how could she tell him that the other man was his only brother? She knew that if she called Ant, he would be there with her, and they could tell Darius together. In her heart, she felt like that would be the safest option. She didn't actually think that Darius would do anything to her; however, she knew hurt people hurt people, and she didn't want to be caught in the crossfire of that.

When Darius returned with her food, she let him know that she wanted to be alone. She needed to just chill out with her thoughts and get herself together. He agreed but let her know he would be back to check on her in the morning. Shanté agreed before going up to her room to relax.

Darius had indeed come that next morning as promised, as well as every day after that for the next two weeks. Shanté had yet to tell Darius that the baby she was carrying wasn't his. She knew she was wrong for not telling him, but she was loving the treatment she was receiving. For the very first time since they'd gotten together, she truly felt love from Darius.

One afternoon, a few days before Christmas, Shanté was lying on the couch, watching Christmas movies, when there was a knock at her door. She opened it to see Ant standing there with a gift bag in hand.

"Can we talk?" Ant asked.

Without a word, Shanté opened the door wider, allowing Ant entry. It had been several weeks since they'd spoken, and she missed him a lot. They both took a seat on the couch, and Ant was the first one to speak.

"I miss y'all. I don't want you or my baby away from me this long again."

Shanté nodded her head in agreement. "We miss you too."

"Look, baby, I was fucking Lashay, but I cut that shit off before we got together. I'm not lying when I say that. It's the truth. She didn't tell me she was pregnant until weeks later. Everyone in the hood knows how Lashay is. I mean, the bitch is fifteen with twins. I honestly don't think the baby she carrying is mine. Hell, that could be the nigga down the street's baby."

"Did you fuck her raw?" Shanté asked, honestly wanting to know.

"Yeah, I did."

"So, then her baby could indeed be yours?"

"I mean, I guess if you put it like that then yes, it could be. But could is a strong word when you talking about being a parent. This baby in you, I know for a fact is mine. So, which do you think I'm going to choose? I love you, Shanté, and I'm not going to allow anything to fuck that up."

"We got to tell Darius that the baby isn't his. He deserves to know what's really been going on," Shanté spoke.

"Shit, call him over. We can have this conversation right now," Ant suggested.

"Nah, let's wait until after Christmas. Yo mama invited me to Christmas dinner, and you know how she been planning it. It's going to be the first time in two years that y'all sister is coming home, and I don't want to ruin that for your mother. We can tell him the day after Christmas so that we can go into the new year without any lies," Shante suggested.

Ant indeed knew how important this Christmas was for his mother. Ant loved to see his mother happy. Ant knew he couldn't prolong the enviable. So, he would wait just a few more days. They sat there together, watching Christmas movies. Ant had even taken a trip to the Coney to pick them both up some wings.

. . .

CHRISTMAS MORNING CAME QUICKLY, SHANTÉ WOKE UP EARLY to put all the gifts she'd gotten for her first niece, Justice, under the tree. Tonya had spent the night so that Justice would be able to wake up with them on Christmas morning. Although she was just a couple months old and wouldn't remember any of this, Shanté still went all out for her, spending several hundred dollars and getting her niece everything she thought was cute. Shanté and Mook's mother, Sandra, had to be to work that morning at ten, so the family was up in the living room early opening gifts. Shanté and Mook's girlfriend, Tonya, were in the kitchen cooking breakfast for the family while Donny Hathaway sang *This Christmas* in the background.

"Damn, I wish I didn't have to go to work. We should be spending Christmas as a family," Sandra stated.

"Shit, call off, Ma. You work enough hours in that place that if you need to take a day then you should be able to," Mook informed, placing Justice in the new pink and white swing Shanté had bought her.

"You right, Mook, but that's not how it works. Holidays are mandatory. If I call off, I'm going to get fired, and I can't afford that. The good thing is that I only have to work one job today, so I will be home around seven. And I'm off tomorrow, so we can still have a Christmas when I get off."

"That's cool, Ma. Tonya is cooking dinner anyway, and you know I got us a few bottles. So, we 'bout to have some fun," Mook confessed.

"What you doing today, Shanté? You gon' be here when I get home?" Sandra asked.

"Darius's mom invited me over there for Christmas dinner. But that's at four. So, if I'm not home by the time you get here, it won't be too long after," Shanté replied.

"Good, so it's settled. Family Christmas begins when I get home from work tonight." Sandra beamed.

They all sat around the table and ate breakfast before Sandra went to work. Later that afternoon, Shanté made her way over to Darius' mother's house for Christmas dinner. He'd suggested that he come pick Shanté up, but she declined, opting to drive herself because she didn't want Ant feeling any type of way.

She pulled up to the huge brick home inside the Palmer Woods community and parked in front. She saw it was beautifully decorated with white lights and huge green and gold wreaths. She grabbed the gift bag that housed the gifts she'd gotten for Mr. and Mrs. Clark and got out the car. As she walked up to the door, she could smell the delicious meal that was being prepared inside. She rang the doorbell and waited to be let inside.

Tamika, Darius and Ant's sister, opened the door and greeted Shanté with a hug. "How you been, girl? Darius told us you were about to give birth to my new little niece or nephew. I'm so excited." Tamika beamed.

"Yeah, I got a little bun in the oven, so you're definitely about to be an aunt." *Your other brother is the father though.* Shanté finished the second part of that statement in her head.

Shanté walked through the house, greeting everyone that was inside, before heading to the kitchen. "Hey, Mrs. Clark. Merry Christmas. Can I help you with anything?" Shanté asked.

"Merry Christmas to you too, Shanté. And how many times do I have to tell you to call me Mama Pat? Now you just sit your pretty self down here and talk to me for a minute." Shanté smiled and took a seat at the kitchen island.

"Darius told me you were pregnant, says you're almost four months now?"

"Yes, that's right," Shanté responded, smiling as she rubbed her stomach.

"Are you ready to be a mother?"

Shanté thought about it for a moment before she answered the question. "I don't think anyone is truly ready to become a parent. But what I will say is that I will love my baby the best. He or she will never want for anything, and I will make sure of that."

"Mama, I know you not in here talking Shanté's ear off, are you?" Darius asked, coming into the kitchen and interrupting their conversation.

He walked over to Shanté, greeting her with a kiss on the cheek. When she looked over, she saw Ant standing in the entryway of the kitchen, watching their interaction. She frowned when their eyes collided, and she felt like she was doing something wrong by letting Darius kiss her.

"Merry Christmas, Ant," she called out, stepping away from Darius.

"Merry Christmas, Shanté."

"Is everyone ready to eat? If so, I can start putting the food out," Mama Pat asked.

Everyone said yes, and Tamika helped her put the turkey, ham, and ribs, along with all the side dishes, on the serving table. They'd just finished bringing everything out when the doorbell rang.

"Oh, that must be my surprise. I'll get it," Mama Pat cheered.

"Surprise? What type of surprise?" Darius asked.

"Well, the surprise is for Anthony, but I think the rest of you will be surprised too," she revealed.

"Look at Ant ass, always the favorite. Mama ain't get the rest of us no surprises but was sure to get her baby boy one," Darius joked.

"Oh, boy, hush that nonsense." Mama Pat laughed with a wave of her hand as she went to open the door. She returned a few moments later with a huge smile on her face.

"Anthony, baby, look who I found."

When Ant looked up to find Lashay walking into the dining room, his face turned from having a pleasant smile to a cold stare. She was standing there in a red velvet dress with her pregnant belly bulging out.

"Mama, what is she doing here?" Ant asked in a no-nonsense tone.

"Who is this girl, Patricia?" Mr. Clark asked, sensing his son's uneasiness.

"This is Anthony's friend, Lashay, and she is joining us for Christmas dinner. Now, let's just all sit around the table as family and enjoy a nice holiday meal," Mama Pat suggested.

"But we all not family," Any blurted out.

"Ant, stop that. I will not have this. She is pregnant with your child, so that indeed makes her family. Now Lashay, you go ahead and make you a plate of whatever you want and take a seat at the table. You have just as much right to be here as everyone else."

"Thank you, Mrs. Clark." Lashay smiled sweetly, walking over to the table and beginning to make her plate. She took a seat at the table, making sure she sat next to an empty seat so that Ant could sit next to her. "Ant, baby, I saved you a seat next to me," Lashay called out, tapping on the chair cushion when she saw Ant walking toward the table.

"Nah, I'm good. I'm gon' sit next to my sister," he replied, taking his seat.

Once Mr. Clark said the grace, they all started to eat. Everyone was eating in silence until Tamika spoke up.

"So, Lashay, how many months are you? Ant didn't tell me he was expecting a child with you."

"That's cause I'm not. That ain't my damn baby," Ant answered quickly.

Shanté couldn't help but to look over at Lashay and snicker. She didn't understand why Lashay was even there. *This thirsty bitch wanna be a part of something so bad. In here actin' like she pregnant by my man. We both pregnant, so I can beat her ass and not go to jail,* Shanté thought.

"Ant, don't do that. It's Christmas, and we having dinner. We both know this is your baby, so why even act like this?" Lashay asked sweetly.

"Exactly, it's Christmas day, so why the hell ain't you at home with the two kids you already have?" Ant shot back.

"Anthony, do not talk like that at this table," Pat yelled out, sick of the back-and-forth.

"Well, what you expect, Mama? You brought her here without even talkin' to me about it. This ain't my baby, Mama, and she knows that shit."

"Boy, this is my damn house. I don't have to talk to you about who I bring in here," Pat yelled, done with her son's disrespect.

"That ain't my baby, Ma! How you just gon' believe her over me?"

"You know what, Ant? I'm sick of you not claimin' my baby. You quick to claim this bitch's baby but not mine? You think this bitch better than me or something?" Lashay yelled, standing to her feet. "Bitch, you ain't better than me. You sitting over there next to one brother while you pregnant by the other. You a dirty ass hoe in real life," she continued to yell, pointing at Shanté.

Shanté looked at her in disbelief. She couldn't believe Lashay had just told her secret in front of everyone.

"Girl, what the fuck you just say?" Tamika asked in confusion.

"Oh, you heard exactly what I said. Darius, you probably think that baby she carrying is yours, but it ain't. Shanté been fuckin' Ant behind yo back for a while now. She the reason Ant not claimin' my baby. And yo ass sitting up here with yo chin up like yo ass ain't wrong as hell."

"Bitch, I should fuck you up!" Shanté yelled, standing to her feet.

"Shanté, why is she saying this shit?" Darius asked.

"Because it's true. That ain't yo baby. Gone tell him, y'all. Don't y'all think it's been a secret long enough?"

"Oh, bitch, I'm about to beat yo ass," Shanté warned before running around the table at Lashay. Ant was able to grab her and stop Shanté before she made any contact with Lashay.

"Let the bitch go, Ant. I been ready to put the paws on this hoe. You was so mad at Peanut for fuckin yo man that you went out and fucked my man. You a dirty ass bitch."

"Hoe, this ain't yo man. That's why you so fuckin' mad. You a jealous ass, bitter bitch. You wanna be me so bad that you tried to come up in here and fuck my shit up?" Shante was enraged, and if Ant let her go, she was going to kill Lashay with her bare hands.

"Jealous? Bitch, jealous of what? You ain't got shit I want!" Lashay yelled, still in her fighting stance.

" Bitch, I got Ant. He loves me, and you hate that. You hate that so much that you trying to pin a whole baby on him. But he know which one of us is carrying his real baby." Shanté was so angry that she didn't notice what she'd said until the words left her mouth.

"So, you pregnant by my fuckin' brother? That's not my baby inside you?" Darius asked, hurt evident in his tone.

"I'm so sorry, Darius. This is not the way it was supposed to come out. We wanted to tell you, and we'd planned to do so tomorrow," Shanté explained.

"Tomorrow? How about that was something you should have fuckin' told me when you first said you was pregnant. Bitch, you dirty as fuck for that!" Darius yelled.

Mr. and Mrs. Clark sat at the table, watching everything unfold, not knowing what to do. This was not the outcome that Pat expected when she invited Lashay to Christmas dinner.

"Alright, nah, bro. You not 'bout to talk to her like that in front of me," Ant scolded.

"Nigga, I will talk to her however the fuck I want to talk to her. This is my bitch."

"No, this is my woman and the mother of my child, and

you will not disrespect her," Ant spoke up, placing Shanté behind him with one hand as he stepped forward.

"Oh, so you made her yo girlfriend but told me you wasn't ready for a relationship? We were supposed to be a family. You, me, and our baby," Lashay cried.

Darius looked at Ant with rage in his eyes. He couldn't believe his own brother would do something so horrible to him. *This nigga knew exactly how I felt about her, and he fucked her? I'm 'bout to fuck this snake ass nigga up.* Before anyone knew it, Darius ran over to Ant, punching him in the face. Ant drew back, punching Darius back, causing him to fall on the table and causing the centerpieces to fall over.

"Ahhhhhh," Pat screamed, jumping up from her seat. "Y'all are brothers, and I will not allow y'all to fight in my house over some chick!" she yelled.

With the sound of their mother's voice, the brothers stopped fighting. They both stood, looking at each other with anger in their eyes. "Lashay, it is time for you to go. You have done enough tonight," Pat announced.

"Oh, so now you on her side too? Fine, I'll go but know that this baby is just as much your grandchild as the one this bitch carrying," Lashay said before storming out.

"Now you two need to sit down and have a real conversation about this. I'm sure if y'all talked, y'all would see this is just some crazy misunderstanding."

"I didn't misunderstand anything. This nigga ain't no brother of mine. This no good ass nigga fucked my girl and got her pregnant. And this no good ass bitch just let him. I ain't got shit to say to neither of you," Darius announced before storming out the house.

"Shanté, are you okay?" Ant asked. She was standing there with tears streaming down her face.

"I need to leave," she whispered before walking out the door.

CHAPTER ELEVEN

It was New Year's Eve, and Shanté sat on the couch with a tub of ice cream and a pack of chocolate chip cookies. Her brother and mother had both gone out for the night, leaving Shanté to bring the new year in alone. She didn't mind though; she would much rather be alone. It was early, around eight, so she still had some time left before she could see the ball drop. So, she decided to watch a movie. Going to On Demand, she flicked through all the different movies she could select from. However, before she could choose one, someone began knocking at her door. Getting up from her comfortable space on the couch, she went to go answer the door.

"Hey, baby, I missed you. I can't keep staying away from you and my baby this long. I brought some barbeque from that spot over on Seven Mile. And I thought we could bring in the new year together as a family," Ant suggested, holding up the bag filled with takeout boxes.

Shanté smiled, letting him inside. He followed Shanté into the kitchen where she grabbed two plates. They each filled their plates with ribs, chicken, mac and cheese, baked beans, candied yams, and potato salad before heading back to the living room.

"You didn't want to go out tonight?" Shanté asked, taking her seat on the couch.

"I'm where I want to be. I want to bring in every new year as a family, just like this, for the rest of my life."

She looked at Ant and smiled. He was everything Shanté wanted in a relationship. Ant was loving and treated her like his queen. Even though Lashay was walking around telling everyone she was pregnant by Ant, Shanté knew that Ant would always put her first. Darius was nothing like that. Where Ant was selfless, Darius was selfish. Where Ant cared about her feelings, Darius played with them, trying to see how far he could push Shanté. Even though she knew they both truly loved her, she knew that Ant was the safer of the two.

"You think we should start pickin' out baby names? I been reading a lot of books, and they say that we should start calling the baby by its name while it's still inside you," Ant suggested.

"But we don't know the gender yet. That appointment is still two weeks away."

"That's fine. We can still come up with names. A boy

name and a girl name. Then when we find out what it is, we will already have a name."

"Yeah, I like that," Shante replied, smiling. "If the baby is a boy, then I'll pick the name, and if it's a girl, then you can pick it," she continued.

"Yeah, that's cool cause it's always Daddy's lil girl."

"Okay, so if it's a boy, I think his name should be Richard Anthony Clark. Richard is my daddy's name, and when he passed, I vowed to name my son after him."

"Yeah, that's cool with me. If it's a girl, I think we should name her Brianna Bonnie Clark," he suggested.

"I actually like that name. I thought you was 'bout to pick somethin' hella crazy." Shanté laughed.

"Nah, I ain't 'bout to let our baby get bullied in school over no crazy ass name."

They sat there, eating barbeque and watching *Poetic Justice*, enjoying each other's company. Ant truly made Shanté happy, and that was all she wanted in a relationship. She was smiling inside and out and loving every minute of it.

"What you wanna watch next?" Ant asked when the movie went off.

"I don't know. You can pick. I gotta go to the bathroom."

Shanté got up and began making her way down the hallway. She'd just gotten to the half bath when she heard the knock at the door. "Ant, can you get that please? I gotta pee so bad," she called out.

"Yeah, I got you, baby," Ant replied, heading to the door.

When he opened it, he was surprised to see Darius standing on the other side. He was holding a bouquet of red roses and a bottle of sparkling cider.

"Nigga, what the fuck you doin here?" Darius scowled.

"I should be asking you the same thing."

"I'm here to see my woman."

"Well, I think that's crazy cause don't no woman of yours live here," Ant shot back.

"Nigga, I ain't 'bout to play these games with you. Where the fuck is Shanté?"

"Look, I know the situation is fucked up, and I know it's hard on you. Hell, it's hard on all of us. We never meant for this shit to happen. But it did, and a baby came out of it. So, now we want to be a family. As hard as it is for you to realize, I love Shanté, and she is my future. Hope one day we can all get past this, and you can accept that."

"Baby, who's at the door?" Shanté asked, returning from the bathroom. Her eyes widened when she saw Darius standing at her door holding flowers. "Darius, what are you doing here?" Shanté asked in surprise.

"I wanted to see you, spend New Years Eve together like we always do. But I see you got my brother here. I guess you don't need me, huh? I would have never thought that you would be sitting around cuddled up with my own brother. Damn, this shit cuttin' a nigga deep, Shanté. I can't lie."

"I'm sorry, Darius. I really don't know what to say. I didn't expect you to come here tonight."

"If I would have come here first, would this nigga still be here?"

Shanté dropped her head low, and Darius already knew the answer. He hated what had become of him and Shanté, but he knew it was all his fault. If he would have never fucked Peanut, none of this would be going on. So, he knew he couldn't be too upset at Shanté. His brother, on the other hand, was a different story. That was supposed to be his blood, and the hurt Ant had caused Darius warranted revenge.

"I get it. You don't have to say it. Don't worry. I'll leave you alone, Shanté," Darius announced before walking off back to his car.

"You okay, baby?" Ant asked as he closed the door.

"Yeah, I'm good. I just hate doing him like that. I know he's hurt by this shit. You're his brother. I didn't mean for none of this to happen."

"Neither one of us meant for this to happen. But I'm not 'bout to apologize for my child, and you shouldn't either. This baby that you are carrying is a blessing to us both."

"You know what? You're right, Ant. It's time for us to think about our family," Shante agreed.

They spent the rest of the night on the couch, watching movies, and they vowed that from that day forward, they would bring in every new year together as a family.

CHAPTER TWELVE

Ant hadn't left Shanté's side her entire pregnancy, and she was loving her new family dynamic. One summer's day when Shanté was eight months pregnant, Ant showed up to her house, letting her know that he had a surprise for her.

"Okay, what is it?" she asked eagerly.

"You gon' have to come with me and see."

"Let me get dressed right quick."

"You look fine. Let's just go," Ant suggested.

Shanté looked down at herself. She had on a pair of gray leggings and an oversized white t-shirt. There was no way she was dressed for any surprise Ant might have. However, before she could protest any further, Ant grabbed her hand and led her out to his car.

"Boy, you bet not be takin' me nowhere that anyone is

gon' see me. I look a fuckin' mess," Shanté spoke, running her hand over her ponytail.

"Relax, baby, you look beautiful."

About fifteen minutes later, they pulled up to a huge brick house on West Outer Drive.

"Whose house is this?" Shanté asked, looking around at the beautiful landscaping.

"It's our house," Ant announced, getting out the car and walking around to open Shanté's door.

"This is our house? Like mine and yours?" Shanté questioned.

"That's right, baby. This is our house, and we gon' raise our beautiful family in this muthafucka."

"Ahhhh," Shanté screamed, jumping up in Ant's arms and hugging him tightly. "I love you so much, baby. Thank you."

" I love you more, and you're welcome. Let's go in so you can take a tour," Ant suggested.

Shanté happily agreed, walking in the home behind Ant, and they walked through every room of the four-bedroom, three-bathroom house that Shanté quickly planned to make their home.

"When can we move in?"

"Shit, today if you want to. We can go shopping right now and get all the furniture we need," Ant informed.

That was exactly what they did. They went to store after store, getting everything they needed to furnish their new home. Ant even paid extra so that everything would be delivered that day.

EVERYTHING WAS WONDERFUL. SHANTÉ AND ANT WERE LIVING together as a couple and were waiting for the arrival of their daughter. One day while they were getting ready to do some last minute baby shopping, Shanté's water broke.

"Oh, shit, babe. I think it's time," Shanté announced as the liquid ran from between her legs and onto the floor.

"Oh, my God, you 'bout to have my baby?" Ant asked, running around the room frantically. "I need my keys. Where the fuck are my keys?" Ant continued to yell.

"Baby, they're right there," Shanté informed, pointing to the coffee table.

Ant turned around, grabbing his keys before getting Shanté's hospital bag out of the closet. Once he was sure they had everything, they made their way to the car, heading to the hospital. Shanté could tell Ant was nervous and so was she. However, she wanted to reassure him that everything would be fine.

"OKAY, SHANTÉ, ON THE COUNT OF THREE, I NEED YOU TO give me a big push," the doctor ordered. As soon as the doctor got to three, Shanté pushed as hard as she could and didn't stop until she heard the soft cries of her baby.

"It's a girl," the doctor announced, placing the baby on Shanté's chest. She cradled her baby as tears rolled down her cheeks.

"Ant, look what we made," Shanté said softly, kissing her baby girl on the top of her head.

"Hey, Brianna. I'm your daddy, and I love you very much. The world is yours, baby girl," Ant whispered, running his hand over Brianna's head full of curly hair.

"She's so beautiful," Shanté admired, looking down at her daughter.

"I love you so much, Shanté. I promise you I'm gonna take care of y'all. It's us against everybody from here on out."

Shanté smiled and kissed Ant softly on the lips, spending the rest of their night together as first time parents.

SHANTÉ WAS FINALLY GETTING DISCHARGED FROM THE hospital, and she couldn't be happier. She was ready to get home and sleep in her bed. She had dressed Brianna in a pink onesie with purple hearts and placed a purple bow on her head. They'd had been in such a rush to get to the hospital that they had left Brianna's car seat at home. When the hospital staff informed them that they wouldn't be able to discharge Brianna without her having a car seat, Ant went back to the house to get it. Shanté sat in the chair in the room with Brianna in her arms as she waited on Ant to return.

Once an hour had come and gone, Shanté decided to call

him and see where he was. When he didn't answer the phone, she figured he was driving back to the hospital.

"I just need you to sign these papers, and once your boyfriend returns with the car seat, you guys can be on your way," the nurse stated as she walked into Shanté's room.

Smiling, Shanté took the papers and the pen and signed all the paperwork the nurse had given her. The hospital was sending them home with a baby bag full of diapers, bottles, and blankets. Her mother had told her to take everything they gave her and to not leave anything at the hospital. So, that was exactly what she did.

"Where the hell are you, Ant?" Shanté said aloud as she looked over at the clock. By now, two hours had passed, and she didn't understand what was taking him so long. With them living only fifteen minutes away from the hospital, she knew that he should have been back by now. She called his phone several more times, and like every time before, he didn't answer. Shanté didn't know what to do as she sat in the hospital with no way home.

Finally, after three hours of waiting, she called Mook. He told her that he still had one of Justice's old car seats at home and would be there soon to pick them up. Shanté didn't know if she was mad at Ant or worried about him. *Why wouldn't he come back?* Shanté thought to herself. When Mook arrived, he packed everything in the car before helping Shanté in the backseat.

"Where is Ant?" Mook asked as he pulled out of the hospital parking lot.

"I don't know. He went home to grab the car seat for the baby. But he never came back. It just don't sound right. Something has to be wrong."

"We can go to your house and see if he there. If not, I'm taking you to Mama's house. I'm not gon' have you home alone with a brand-new baby," Mook informed.

Shanté nodded her head, knowing that a debate with her brother was something she couldn't win. She knew Mook was only going to do what he thought was best for her. So, she just sat back in the seat without saying another word.

When they pulled up to the house, everything seemed to be in place. Mook went inside to check everything out. Although he didn't see any sign of Ant, he did see the pink car seat still sitting by the door, letting him know that Ant hadn't come to get it. *I know this nigga bet not have left my sister with a damn baby,* Mook thought to himself.

He walked back out to the car, letting Shanté know she would have to come pack a bag for her and the baby.

"He not in there?" Shanté asked.

"Nah, and the car seat is still sitting by the door."

Shanté got out the car and allowed Mook to grab Brianna. She walked inside, still sore from just giving birth. She could tell that Ant hadn't come back to get the car seat. She didn't want to stay at her mother's house, but she knew her brother wouldn't allow her to stay at home. However, she asked anyway.

"I think I'ma be good. We can stay here. Ant will be home soon, especially after he goes back to the hospital and see I'm not there."

"Nah, sis, I'm taking you to Mama's house. What if that nigga don't come back? You just gon' be here alone?" Mook knew his sister would need to take it easy after having a baby. There was no way she could do that and take care of a baby by herself. So, he felt like their mother's house would be the best place for her.

"Why wouldn't he come back?" Shantè asked, confused.

"Shit. I don't know. Why would he leave y'all at the hospital for so long with no way home? Why would he tell you he was going to get a car seat that he never came to get? I got questions just like you. But what it looks like is this nigga got scared to be a father and bounced."

"What? Hell nah, that can't be it. Ant was happy that we had become parents together. Last night, we talked about all the memories we would make with our daughter. Something had to happen, Mook." Shanté tried to convince him.

Mook looked into his sister's eyes. He knew she wanted desperately to believe that Ant hadn't just made her a single mother, no matter how many signs pointed to the fact that he'd done just that. However, he agreed to start calling nearby hospitals and police stations, just to see if Ant was possibly in any of them. Just like Mook thought, he wasn't.

"Pack y'all a bag so we can go. I gotta be at work in an hour," Mook ordered.

ANT WALKED OUT OF THE HOSPITAL, EAGER TO GET THE CAR seat and get back to the hospital. Ant was excited about their daughter coming home for the first time. He'd just gotten into his car when his cell phone rang.

"What up doe?" Ant answered without paying attention to who was calling.

"415 Hoover Street," the unidentified caller spoke.

"Fuck you say? Who the fuck is this?" Ant yelled into the phone, confused about who would be calling him, repeating his address.

"Yo bitch at Oakwood Hospital, room 312? She just had yo baby, right?" the man replied.

"Nigga, you better leave my family the fuck outta this. Who the fuck are you, and what do you want?"

"If you want yo so called family to be safe, then you will meet me on the corner of Fort and Junction in twenty minutes."

The call ended, leaving Ant confused. *If I want to keep my family safe? Like, nigga, you would do something to them if I don't come meet you? Fuck is this shit about?* Ant thought to himself as he headed toward 94, making it to his destination in record time. As soon as his car parked on the corner, his phone rang.

"Get out the car and walk down the alley."

"Nigga, what? I ain't doing that shit," Ant replied.

"Do it, nigga. Or yo girl and baby die. You wouldn't want that, now would you?"

Ant hesitated for a few seconds before getting out the car. He wasn't strapped because he'd just left the hospital. So, he had nothing but his hands to defend himself. He cautiously walked down the alley, looking over his shoulders every few steps. His phone rang again, and the same man told him to walk into the door of the abandoned warehouse when he got to the dead end. Ant did as he was instructed, and as soon as he got inside the building, gunshots rang out. He tried to duck, but there was nothing in his line of sight that he could hide behind. Shot after shot sounded off, and Ant could see his entire life flash before his eyes. Then, all of a sudden, the gunfire stopped.

"You see how scared you just were when them bullets started flying? How scared do you think Shanté would be?" The man's voice echoed.

"Man, what you on? Fuck is this about?" Ant yelled out.

"This is about the family you claim to love keeping their lives. That's what you want, right? To keep your family alive?"

The man stepped into view, leaving Ant even more confused. Standing before him was a tall, dark-skinned man with a short haircut. Ant had never seen the man before in his life and didn't understand how he knew so much about him.

"Who the fuck are you?" Ant asked.

"The man that will kill your family if you don't agree to leave town tonight."

"Leave town? Nigga, is you crazy? I'm not leaving my girl and baby nowhere. They coming with me."

"Then you will all die. Ant, this is no joke. I was hired and paid very well to make sure this happens. So, unless you comply, your girl and baby are dead."

"Nigga, you think I'm some kind of pussy or something? I'm not leaving my family nowhere," Ant challenged, calling the man's bluff.

With one nod of his head, the man raised his gun and shot Ant in the arm, causing him to yell out in pain. "I've told you what was going to happen. Now it's up to you to do what you gon' do."

"If I leave, how do I know that you won't just kill them anyway?"

"Because that's not what I'm getting paid to do. As long as you leave, your family is safe," the man responded. "You have to leave now. Don't tell them anything, don't go back to your house. Just get on the road and go. We have eyes everywhere, as you can see. So, at any point, if you go against what we agreed on, we will know. And you already know what would happen then."

Ant was hurt to say the least. There was nothing he wouldn't do for Shanté and Brianna, and if leaving them would keep them safe, then he would do so. Needless to say, Ant agreed to the man's terms and left Detroit.

OVER THE NEXT SEVERAL MONTHS, SHANTÉ SLIPPED INTO A deep depression. There were times she couldn't even get out of bed, forcing her mother to care for Brianna. She didn't understand how Ant could just leave them without telling her anything. She'd not been back to the house she shared with him since the day she left the hospital. Mook had taken it upon himself to go over there and gather all of Shanté and Brianna's belongings and take everything back to their mother's house.

One day while Shanté was sitting on the couch in her robe, the doorbell rang. At first, she wasn't going to answer it but decided to see who it was after the doorbell rang a second time. She opened the door to see Darius standing on the other side.

"What are you doing here, Darius? Are you here to give me some news about Ant?" Shanté asked.

"Nah, we haven't heard from him either. I'm not sure what's up with that. I don't understand. There is nothing in this world that could have made me leave my girl and newborn child. I guess he just wasn't ready."

Although Shanté hated to admit it, she was starting to think that it was true. Everyone around her told her that Ant had up and left them. At first, she didn't believe it, but now, she was starting to see things differently.

"Can I come in?" Darius asked.

Shanté nodded her head and opened the door wider before walking back to the couch.

"How are you and Brianna doing?"

"We're okay. I'm just taking things one day at a time."

"How 'bout you go get dressed and let me take you out to lunch? Maybe some time away would do you some good," Darius suggested.

"Nah, I'm okay. I don't have anyone to watch the baby."

"Bullshit! Girl, if you don't go get dressed. You know damn well I'm gonna watch my granddaughter. Go get dressed. You need to get out this house. You been in here sad for months. Go have some damn fun." Shanté heard her mama call from the kitchen.

She knew her mother meant well, but she wasn't in the mood to go anywhere. What she wanted was to be a family with Ant and their daughter. However, it was clear to her that what she wanted didn't matter.

"Let me go get dressed," Shanté responded.

DARIUS TOOK SHANTÉ TO A MEXICAN RESTAURANT HE KNEW she loved. However, instead of eating inside, he placed a carryout order.

"Where we going?" Shanté asked.

"You'll see," Darius spoke, not taking his eyes off the road.

A few moments later, they were turning down the Belle Isle bridge. Darius drove until he found a quiet spot with no other people around. He parked, getting out of the car and opening the back door.

"What are you doing?" Shanté asked, watching Darius grab a blanket from his backseat.

"We're about to have a picnic under that tree right there." Darius pointed.

Shanté couldn't help but smile. It had been the first time in over three months, but there she was, smiling. When her and Darius were together, they would have picnics once a week in the summer, and she always enjoyed them. It had been time for her to enjoy food and clear her mind. Darius knew Shanté like the back of his hand, so he knew that was exactly what she needed.

"Thank you for this, Darius. This was so sweet."

"It's no problem, Shanté. I know things didn't work out between us, but I will always love you. I want you to know that I'm here for you. If nothing else, you have my niece. My brother is wherever the fuck he is, and you're alone. I can't have that. So, I want you to know if it's anything y'all need, no matter what it is, you can call me."

"Thank you, Darius. That means a lot. I know this can't be easy for you. But even knowing that, you still want to be here to help. That's real love," Shanté replied.

"That's just facts. Somebody gotta be there, and we see it ain't gon' be my weak ass brother."

"You really haven't heard from him?"

Shanté didn't understand what went wrong in such a short time. One moment, they were talking about their future and everything they were going to do as a family. Then, the next minute, he was nowhere to be found. The rejection hurt more than anything because she thought Ant would always choose her, but instead, he was gone, leaving her to raise their child alone. She wondered if this was how Lashay felt when Ant began denying her child.

"Hell nah. I would have told you if I did. That nigga done went ghost."

"See, that's the scary part to me. What if something happened to him?" Shanté asked, becoming teary eyed.

"Shanté, ain't nothing wrong with that nigga. If something happened to him, the streets would have been talking. I know that for sure. That nigga somewhere livin' it up without a care in the world."

Shanté's eyes burned as her tears flowed freely. She knew everything Darius was saying was true. Everyone in the hood knew who Ant was, so if something had happened to him, someone would know. *Damn, this nigga really left me and our baby. How could he do that shit to me?* Shanté thought.

"I'm sorry this happened, Shanté, all of this. I can't help but to think this is all my fault. If I would have never fucked yo cousin, you wouldn't be sitting here crying over my brother," Darius apologized.

"Thank you, Darius. Your apology means a lot. I want you

to know that I'm sorry too. I shouldn't have had sex with your brother. That was out of pocket. But I love my daughter, and I can't apologize for having her. Without him, she wouldn't be here."

"I feel you. I love my niece, and I don't expect an apology for her. And I didn't bring you out here to talk about this. You out here crying when I was trying to put a smile on your face. Let's just eat and enjoy this time away from the drama."

"I feel that. Let's just chill," Shanté replied. They spent the rest of the day under the tree, eating and talking. Shanté really enjoyed her day out of the house and was very thankful that Darius had even thought to do this for her.

CHAPTER THIRTEEN

Five years had passed with no word from Ant at all. Darius had now stepped up, taking on the role of Brianna's father. With her being only a couple days old when Ant left, the only person she knew as daddy was Darius. Shanté had sold the house that Ant had bought for them, and Darius had purchased a new one for them near the Boston Edison district. Life was great, and they were even talking about marriage.

One day, Brianna begged Shanté and Darius to take her to the park. Darius, who always gave in to whatever Brianna wanted, packed up a few snacks while Shanté got Brianna dressed. They made it to the park a few moments later. They sat on the bench as they watched Brianna play. Neither of them noticed themselves being watched.

"She gonna be sleepy as hell when she gets back to the house. You wanna have some adult play time?" Darius asked.

"Hell yeah, it's been a week. I can't remember the last time we went this long."

"Good, maybe we can work on giving Brianna a little brother or sister," Darius suggested, only half joking.

"Boy, now you know you tried it. Brianna is a handful, and as much as I want more kids, I know that now is not the time. I got shit I want to do, and it's a lot with just having Brianna. Let's just wait until she gets a little older."

"Yeah, you right. I don't mind waiting. I'm happy with the family I got."

In the split second they'd taken their eyes off of Brianna, a man had walked up to her and began talking to her. When Darius noticed, he immediately ran up to Brianna, picking her up quickly.

"Nigga, get your weird ass outta here. What kinda grown ass nigga sits here and holds a conversation with a little girl? Do you know who I am? I ain't nothing to play wit'. I'll kill you 'bout mine," Darius threatened.

"You gon' kill 'bout yours? Ain't shit yours over this way. It's all mines, and you know that. I see what yo ass tryin' to do," Ant informed, looking Darius directly in the eyes.

"Ant? What the fuck are you doing here? I thought you were…"

"You thought I was what?" Ant said, cutting Darius off mid-sentence. "You ain't think shit," he continued. "You seen yo chance, and you went for it. I see exactly what you did," Ant continued.

"Daddy, who is this man?" Brianna asked.

"Daddy, huh?" Ant spoke through clenched teeth.

Before Darius could respond, Shanté walked up. When her eyes collided with Ant's, she felt as though the wind had been knocked out of her. She couldn't believe he was standing in front of her, living and breathing. *This muthafucka wasn't hurt, and he left us? How can he just show up here after all this time?*

"Shanté, I've missed you so much," Ant uttered, caressing her cheek softly. His touch alone sent shivers through Shanté's body. She'd missed him tremendously. Not a day had gone by that she hadn't thought about him and what they could have been.

"It's no need to have missed my woman. I don't know what type of games you thought you could play, but someone had to be the adult around here. Let's go, Shanté."

Darius grabbed her hand, and the three of them walked off. Shanté couldn't help but look back at Ant. He'd been gone so long that Shanté thought he was dead. Yet he was just standing in front of her. She'd felt his touch, and that was something she'd yearned for since the day he'd left.

"I can't believe that nigga just showed the fuck up after five fuckin' years. He got some fucking nerve!" Darius yelled. They had just walked into their home, and he was upset their family day at the park had been ruined. "That nigga crazy if he think he just gon' walk back in y'all lives like nothing ever happened. I'm not having this shit."

"Babe, he's Brianna's father. She deserves to know who he is. We can't just keep him away from her."

"I am her father, Shanté. I'm the one that's been there every day with her. I saw her first steps and heard her first words. She calls me daddy because I am the only daddy she knows. That's his fault. But what he not 'bout to do is come in and confuse her."

Shanté knew that this was a lot for Darius. Hell, it was a lot for her too. She never expected to see Ant again, and now there he was. No matter what Darius said, Shanté knew she had to speak with him. She needed to know why he left for her own peace of mind. There would have been nothing that would have made Shanté leave him. She just wanted to know why he hadn't felt the same.

"That nigga can go right back to wherever the fuck he been at for the past five years. He not about to come in here and fuck up the family I've built," Darius announced, clearly enraged.

Shanté felt bad for him, but she wanted him to see things from her position. No matter how hurt she was by Ant's actions, the fact still remained that he was Brianna's father.

"I need to go clear my head. I'll be back later," Darius enlightened before storming out the house.

Shanté was in shambles as tears streamed down her face. She didn't understand how things ended up this way. Once she found out she was pregnant, she'd planned to have a beautiful life with Ant. However, he clearly didn't want that. *What's the point of him coming back now?*

OVER THE NEXT FEW DAYS, THINGS WERE A BIT ROCKY FOR Shanté on the home front. Darius barely spoke to her, and when he did, he was very short with his conversation. He was making her feel like she was doing something wrong, and Shanté didn't like that. She was a victim in Ant's game, and she wanted Darius to see that.

It was a Saturday afternoon, and Shanté was home watching cartoons with Brianna. Darius had left a few hours earlier, not even telling Shanté where he was going. The doorbell rang, and Shanté went to answer it. Much to her surprise, Ant was standing on the other side of the door.

"Damn, you moved out the house I bought us and everything. You was really trying to erase me, huh?" Ant asked in a low tone.

"What are you doing here, Ant? Darius would go crazy if he knew you were here."

"Well, let that muthafucka go crazy then. I came here to get my family back."

"Ant, it's been five years. You think you can just come back and I'm going to welcome you with open arms? You left me. You left our daughter. How could you do that?"

Tears began to stream down Shanté's face, and Ant

dropped his head low. He knew she was hurt, but he needed to explain what happened. He would have never left Shanté if it wasn't for her own safety, and Ant needed for her to understand that.

"Can I come in so that we can talk?"

"No the fuck you cannot. You can get the fuck away from my doorstep though," Darius said from behind Ant, startling Shanté. She had been so caught up in the fact that Ant was standing in her doorway that she hadn't seen Darius pull up.

"Look, Darius, you really don't have anything to do with this. This right here is between me and Shanté. I have to talk to her, not you."

Darius walked closer to Ant, his face etched with anger. "Get the fuck off my doorstep and away from my woman before shit gets ugly," Darius threatened.

"Nah, I ain't gon' let you start no shit with my daughter sitting in there. You would love that, huh? Making me look like the bad guy. You not even worth it. Shanté, we can just talk later," Ant suggested.

"Y'all not gon' talk at all. Your time to talk was five years ago, the day you left. You gave up the rights to your family back then. This my family now, and they good without you," Darius chastised.

Ant didn't say another word to Darius, just nodded his head and walked away.

"Mommy, who is that man?" Brianna asked.

Shanté had been so caught up in what was going on that

she didn't even notice Brianna standing at the door. *I wonder how much she heard?* Shanté thought to herself as she scooped Brianna into her arms.

"That's my brother, Ant. He's your uncle," Darius announced before Shantè could say anything else.

If looks could kill, Darius would have been dead twice over from the way Shanté cut her eyes at him. *How dare this nigga say that to her? It was not his place to tell her anything about Ant.*

"Brianna, baby, why don't you go upstairs and play with your toys while I get you some ice cream? I'll even let yet you eat it in your room," Shanté suggested.

"Yayyyyy, I love ice cream," Brianna cheered, making her way up the stairs. Shanté watched her until she was sure she was in her room and out of earshot.

"Why the fuck would you tell her Ant was her uncle?" Shanté whispered.

"Because he is. I would rather that nigga not come around at all, but if he's going to be around, then she will only know him as her uncle. He missed his chance for him to be anything other than that."

"How is that up to you to decide? Brianna is my child," Shanté shot back.

"Brianna is our child, or did you forget? She calls me daddy, and I have been the only man that has been in her life as a father since she was born. So, now after that nigga abandoned you and her, you want to allow him to uproot her entire life? Did you forget that he already had a child that he wants nothing to do with? My brother is not a man. He's a little boy that is scared to grow up. Let me ask you this. What's going to happen if you tell her that I'm really not her father and Ant is, only for him to disappear again? If he did it once, he's going to do it again. So, what you gon' do then? Allow her to grow up without a father?"

Shanté didn't know what to say. She knew Darius was right. If she told Brianna Darius wasn't her father, what would she think? Darius had been in her life since birth. When Ant left, Darius stepped up and took on the role of Brianna's father, and that was something she couldn't take away from him. *Could I even trust Ant to be a father to Brianna?*

"Let's just allow him to be her uncle for now. That way if he leaves, she won't be disappointed. Then when she gets old enough to understand, then we can talk about telling her the truth."

"You're right. I don't want him to be coming in and out of her life," Shanté agreed.

CHAPTER FOURTEEN

It had been two weeks since Ant had showed up to Darius and Shanté's house, and she hadn't heard from him since. It was a Friday morning, and she was on her way to take Brianna to school. She walked outside and noticed a piece of paper on her windshield. Opening the folded note, she read it and realized it was from Ant.

Meet me at our spot at eleven this morning... Ant.

Shanté quickly folded the note back up, putting it in her pocket before Darius noticed it. He brought Brianna outside and placed her in her booster seat before kissing her on the forehead.

"Have a good day at school, baby. Daddy's gon' come get you when you get out."

"And take me to McDonald's?" Brianna asked.

"If McDonald's is what my princess wants then that's what my princess gets."

"Yayyyy, I love McDonald's. I can't wait to get out of school," Brianna cheered.

"I got some errands to run, so I'll be back later," Shanté informed.

Darius walked around to the driver's side door before planting a kiss on Shanté's lips. "Okay, cool. Tonight, I'ma give my queen what she wants," Darius said with a wink.

"Yeah, I'ma need that," Shanté replied, licking her lips.

She drove off, dropping Brianna off at school. She still had a couple hours before she was to meet Ant, but she knew if she went home first, she would have to explain to Darius what she was doing. Darius had become very insecure since Ant had come back, and she didn't feel like arguing with him. So, she decided she would just sit inside the parking lot of the restaurant until she saw him pull in.

DARIUS HAD SEEN ANT PLACE THE NOTE ON SHANTÉ'S windshield. His camera system alerted him the moment someone stepped on his property. The moment Ant pulled off, Darius went outside and read the note.

"This meeting will never happen," Darius spoke aloud as he folded the note back up. He placed the note back on Shanté's windshield and walked back into the house.

That next morning when Shanté pulled off to take Brianna to school, Darius placed a call.

"Hello?" the man answered.

"We didn't get rid of my problem the way we thought. He's back now and trying to pick up where he left off. That nigga has got to go," Darius informed him.

"Five years ago, I told him to never come back if he wanted his woman and child safe. Since he is now back, am I to kill them?"

"Hell no, you are not to touch my family. No harm should come to them at all. It is him that you are to kill. Take him out and the reward will be great," Darius ordered.

"Do you have a location for him?"

"I will send it over to you. Make sure you handle it."

Darius got off the phone and texted the location of the restaurant. He was ready for this to come to an end. There was no way he was going to allow Ant to come and take his family from him. Knowing the only way to stop Ant from doing so was death, Darius put a price on his head, not feeling remorseful at all about Ant being his own brother.

ANT MADE HIS WAY DOWN WAYNE ROAD, READY TO SEE Shanté. He was going to tell her everything. He wanted her to know that he didn't just abandon her and their daughter. He would have never left if he didn't think that was the only way to keep them safe. Their safety was his only priority, and he hoped Shanté would understand that.

He came to a stop at a red light, thinking about how Shanté would respond to everything he was going to tell her. He prayed she would forgive him and see things from his point of view. He prayed that he would get a chance to be in his daughter's life. As much as he wanted to be with Shanté, he would understand if she chose to continue to be with Darius. All he wanted was a relationship with his daughter. The light turned green, and he pulled off, not noticing the car that was following him.

Ant was about a mile from his destination when he was cut off by a black SUV. Swerving to avoid hitting the SUV, he hit the curb and ran into a tree. Blood poured from his head, and he could barely stay awake. His door opened, and Ant was dragged from the car. He was so dazed from the accident that he didn't even fight the man as he inserted the syringe, causing Ant to lose consciousness instantly.

Shanté sat at the restaurant, waiting for Ant to arrive. She was eager to have this conversation with him. She had a lot of unanswered questions, and she needed Ant to answer them. She'd been in the dark long enough, and it was now time for Ant to allow her to step into the light. She sat at the table, looking out the window, wanting to see Ant before he saw her. *I wonder what he's going to say? What could he say? What would be a good reason for someone to abandon their family for five years?*

"Are you ready to order?" the waitress asked, breaking Shanté away from her thoughts.

"I'm waiting on someone, but you can bring me a cup of coffee for now."

"I'll get that right to you. Then I'll come back when the rest of your party arrives to take your order."

Shanté nodded her head and watched as the waitress walked away, bringing her coffee back a few moments later. She continued to sit at the table, sipping her coffee while she waited. About fifteen minutes later, the waitress was back at the table.

"I'm still waiting, but I guess I will order for myself," Shanté informed as she looked over the menu.

When her food arrived and Ant was still not there, she began to feel stupid. *How could I let this nigga play me again? If he not here by the time I finish my food, that nigga will never get another chance with me. I'm not playing these fucking games anymore,* Shanté thought to herself.

When Shanté finished her food, she paid her tab before walking back to her car. She was upset, but not with Ant. She was madder at herself for allowing Ant to do this to her for a second time. She would be damned if he would continue to run away from being a father. "My daughter don't need yo ass. She has a good daddy in her life," Shanté spoke aloud before pulling out of the parking lot.

. . .

DARIUS SAT IN THE LIVING ROOM WITH A GLASS OF Hennessey in his hand. Although it wasn't even noon, Darius needed the drink. His life was spiraling out of control, and he needed to get a handle on it before he lost all control. His phone rang, and he picked it up on the first ring, hoping it was Mario.

"Darius, we have a problem," Mario spoke into the phone.

"You didn't get him, did you?"

"No, I got him. Brought him back to the spot and everything. But somehow, he got away. I've searched everywhere for him, and he's not here."

"What the fuck you mean he got away? Find him!" Darius yelled.

"I tried, but he's gone, D," Mario informed.

"Nigga, you had one fuckin' job, and you couldn't even do it. Does he know who you are or that I'm involved in this?"

"I don't think so. He was out once I got him, and I never said your name."

"I can't believe you fucked this up." Darius didn't waste any more time talking. His anger was through the roof, and all he could do was end the call.

This nigga 'bout to take my family away from me. And I'm gon' have to kill him, Darius thought to himself as he downed his drink. He'd paid a great deal of money to have Ant dealt with, and unfortunately, he'd just wasted it.

. . .

Ant stood outside the open window of the house as he listened to the conversation. He couldn't believe his own brother had set him up like this. As he peeked into the window, he looked at the man. It was the same man that had threatened to kill Shanté and Brianna if he didn't leave. *Darius planned all this shit. This weak ass nigga wanted my family so fucking bad,* Ant thought to himself before taking off running down the street.

CHAPTER FIFTEEN

It had been an entire year since the day Shanté was supposed to meet Ant, and she had yet to hear from him. She'd vowed to herself never to allow Ant to play her or her daughter again. So with that, she told Darius that he would continue to play the role as Brianna's father, letting him know that if Ant wanted to be in Brianna's life, she would only know him as her uncle. Darius was happy with the news because he knew his plan had worked. Darius had gotten exactly what he wanted, and nobody even knew he was behind everything that happened — or so he thought.

One Saturday morning, Brianna woke up early. She went into her parents' room to wake up Shanté. She was hungry, and it was time for her Saturday morning pancakes. She'd just walked into her parents' room when she heard a loud voice calling for her father.

"Darius Clark, this is the Detroit police. Come out with your hands up!" the voice called out.

Shanté jumped up the moment she heard the voice. She looked around sleepily, thinking she might have been dreaming. However, when she heard the voice again, she knew she wasn't.

"Darius Clark, if you do not come out, we will come in."

Jumping out of bed, Shanté screamed Darius' name as she grabbed Brianna up into her arms.

"Darius, get up! The police are outside the house!" she yelled.

"What? What are you talking about? Outside for what?" he asked, rubbing his sleepy eyes.

"The police outside," she repeated.

Before Darius could reply, he heard them outside. "I repeat, if you do not come out, we will come in. This is the Detroit police. Come out with your hands up."

"Fuck they want with me?" Darius asked, jumping up and slipping on a pair of sweatpants and a white T-shirt. He quickly ran down the stairs and opened the front door with his hands held high. There were four police cars and a SWAT truck outside of his house, and he had no clue what was going on. Two uniformed officers walked up to him, and one put him in handcuffs while reading him his rights.

"What the fuck am I being arrested for?" Darius asked, confused.

"Capitol murder," one of the officers answered while the other walked him to the patrol car.

"Fuck are you talkin' 'bout? I ain't kill nobody."

Without saying another word, the officer placed Darius into the car. Darius watched as the officers and detectives walked into his home. *Fuck is going on? They got the wrong fuckin' person,* Darius thought to himself as he looked out the window.

He saw Shanté and Brianna being walked out of their home in their pajamas. All he wanted to do was run to them and tell them it would be okay, but he couldn't. He was handcuffed and locked inside of a police car. They sat down on the porch, and Darius watched as Shanté called someone on her cell phone. He saw the tears streaming down her face as she spoke to whoever she'd called. Several moments later, Mook's car pulled up, and he got out, damn near running to Shanté and pulling her into a hug.

"What the fuck is going on?" Mook asked Shanté.

"I don't know. The police say he's being arrested for murder. But I don't know who they trying to say he killed. They in there fuckin' my house up. And my daughter gotta see all this shit," Shanté cried.

"Come on. I'm taking you back to my house. We can come back once the police are done, and I'll help you clean up," Mook suggested.

"Hell no! I'm not leaving my home in their hands. I don't trust these muthafuckas at all. I could come back, and they could have taken everything that belongs to me. I just need you to take Brianna while this shit is going on. I will come over after they leave."

Mook nodded his head, understanding where his sister was coming from. "Come on, Bri. Let's go back to my house and get you dressed. I'm taking you and Justice to Chuck E. Cheese."

"Chuck E. Cheese? It's so much fun there! Yayyyyy." Brianna beamed.

Mook held out his hand, and Brianna grabbed it before jumping off her mother's lap. They walked to the car, and Mook put Brianna inside before they pulled off.

When Shanté was finally allowed back in her home four hours later, it looked like a tornado had ran through it. Everything was thrown off of every desk, table, and counter and onto the floor. Her couches were turned over, and the mattresses and box springs were off the frames. All she could do was shake her head at the mess she had to clean up.

She had no clue what to do since she and Darius had never discussed this even happening. Grabbing her phone, she placed a call to Darius' mother, letting Ms. Pat know that Darius had been arrested. Thankfully for Shanté, Ms. Pat had a lawyer who she could call on Darius' behalf.

"Don't worry, sweetheart. Darius will be home before you know it," Ms. Pat assured before ending the call.

Shanté then made a call to Mook, letting him know that she was back in the house and all the police were gone. She informed him of the condition they'd left the house in and asked if he could keep Brianna for the night. He agreed, and Shanté began straightening up the mess the police had made.

Over the next two years, Darius was in court every few months. They had denied him bail due to the severity of his charges. There was an extreme amount of evidence against him, and Darius didn't understand how. He didn't even know the people he was being accused of murdering. So, he had no clue how they had any type of evidence against him. It was clear to him that he was being set up, but nobody would listen to him.

"My best advice to you would be to take the plea deal they're offering. You could do the thirty years they suggest or continue to go to trial and be in prison for the rest of your life," his lawyer informed.

"I'm not taking no fucking plea for something I didn't do. I'm telling you somebody is setting me up. You my fuckin' lawyer. You should be listening to me."

"I am listening to you, Mr. Clark. However, I feel like you're not listening to me. Unless you can tell me who set you up, and we can prove they really committed the crimes, there is nothing we can do. They have been looking over this case for years, and all the evidence points to you. We could take this to trial if you would like. That is your right; however, I can't see it going well for you if we do."

"I'll take my chances at trial. I'm not admitting to shit I ain't do."

Darius was sentenced to fifty years in prison without the possibility of parole. After a year of being in prison, he received a letter one day. The letter was from Ant but had no return address on it. *Damn, I would have never thought this nigga would be sending me letters,* Darius thought as he opened the envelope.

DARIUS,

I never thought I would be writing these words to you, my big brother. When we were kids, I used to want to be just like you. But boy have them tables turned. As I sit here with this steak dinner in front of me, I savor the sweet taste of revenge. You tried to kill me because I had the one thing you didn't, a family. I would have never thought you would have tried to kill a nigga, even threatened the lives of the two people you claimed to have loved. But we all know that bitch, Karma, had to come back around. You a bitch ass nigga, bro, and you know what they do to bitch ass niggas in prison. Don't worry though. My family will be well taken care of.

. . .

DARIUS WAS LIVID AS HE READ THE LETTER. HE BALLED THE paper up in his hand as he realized that Ant had been the one to set him up. He bit his bottom lip and flared his nostrils, trying not to explode. All this time, Darius had been playing checkers while Ant was playing chess. He knew there was nothing he could do about it now, so he would spend the rest of his time in prison, wishing he'd done things differently.

CHAPTER SIXTEEN

"Ma, why did you wait so long to tell me all this?" Brianna asked, looking over at Shanté. This was the first time they'd talked, and Shanté's story had Brianna's mouth wide open.

"I didn't know how to tell you any of this. You were a daddy's girl. You always wanted to be around him, and Darius would go to the ends of the earth for you. I couldn't be the one to rip that away from you. Even with him being in prison, he never missed a beat. I couldn't promise that Ant would do the same thing." Shanté dropped her head low, feeling sad as she reminisced. "I was so mad at Ant that I didn't even want him around. As much as I loved that man, I hated him. He abandoned us two days after you were born. And for five years. Then, when I tried to give him a chance, he didn't even show up to explain himself. I knew that's how it would always be. If

I would have told you the truth, then it would have been all bad. Not only would I have been taking a good father out of your life, I would have been replacing him with a nigga that would have been in and out every five years. I just couldn't do that to you. At the time, I thought it was the right thing to do. He wouldn't even take care of Lashay's daughter. And he had already showed me what it was with me and him," Shanté admitted.

"But Ma, it wasn't even his fault. Darius did that. So, if it wasn't for him, Ant would have been there."

"You're right, and that's where I fucked up at. I didn't even know about any of that until the day before Ant was murdered. Your father — I mean, Darius — called me one night, saying he was trying to turn over a new leaf and had some things he needed to get off his chest. He said the shit had been heavy on his heart, and he needed to come clean, and that's when he told me. I had planned to go to Ant and apologize, but he died before I could. That shit right there is what's gon' fuck me up forever. Ant loved me, and it wasn't until that day that I realized it. He loved you too. I can't imagine how he felt for nineteen years, and he never once said anything. I know that was because he wanted to keep you happy, even if it hurt him."

"Damn, I wish I could have gotten to know him as my dad because he was a cool ass uncle. But Ma, do you think Dominique was really his daughter?" Brianna asked.

"Honestly baby, I don't know. I do know that Lashay and

Ant were messing around close to the time she got pregnant. But I also know how Lashay got around. She looked exactly like Lashay too, so no matter who her father was, she had none of his features. So, that's just something that we will never know."

ASPEN TOSSED AND TURNED IN THE BED, TEARS STREAMING down her face uncontrollably. She felt like her entire world was lost, and she had no clue how to find it. The past two years of her life had been an entire lie, and she didn't even see it. She couldn't even mourn the death of a man she'd loved so much because he never had love for her. She was a revenge plot for him. He was sent to set her up to die, and it had almost happened. She was carrying the child of a man that wanted her dead, and it hurt.

Placing her hand on her stomach, she rubbed it. She didn't know the first thing about being a mother. *How can I bring a baby into all this chaos? What would I even tell my baby about its father? Damn, I wish my mama was here. She would know exactly what I should do.* Aspen's mind was all over the place. However, the one thing she knew for sure was that she was going to keep her baby. Aspen cried herself to sleep that night, thinking about all the good times she'd had with Quan. Even though it had all been a lie, the memories brought her comfort.

. . .

THAT NEXT AFTERNOON, ASPEN ACCOMPANIED BRIANNA AND Shanté to the hospital to see Justice. Shanté had been worried about her niece since she'd found out what happened. Even though Brianna and Aspen assured her that Justice was doing good, Shanté needed to see for herself. When the three of them walked into the hospital room, Justice was sitting up in her bed, talking to Cream.

"Hey, y'all. I'm glad to see y'all. Auntie, how you doing?" Justice asked, seeing the bruises on her face. Shanté had attempted to hide them with makeup; however, Justice could still see them.

"I'm okay. I'm more worried about you. You're the one that's been shot."

"I'm good now. They said I was messed up for a minute, but you know I'ma bounce back," Justice announced.

"I'm glad you did," Shanté spoke.

"Are you in any pain, Justice?" Brianna asked.

"Nah, not right now. They got me on a lot of medications, so I don't feel nothing right now. I'm just glad y'all okay."

"Shit, we glad you're okay," Shanté replied.

"I'm glad we all okay," Brianna reiterated.

"Aspen, you good?" Justice asked, noticing her friend was staring off into space. She hadn't spoken a word since she'd walked into Justice's room. So, she knew something was off.

When Aspen burst into tears, Cream got up from his seat, letting Justice know that he would give them time to talk.

Shanté also left the room, informing them that she was going to visit Tonya. When the room was clear, Justice asked again.

"What you feeling, Aspen?"

"I'm pregnant," she announced.

Justice's mouth dropped. Cream had already told her what happened and that Quan was involved as well. So, she knew her friend was going through it, and she hated that for her.

"It's gonna be okay. We gonna get through this shit the same way we get through everything together," Justice assured.

"Right! You know we got you, Aspen. We gonna be there every step of the way," Brianna guaranteed.

"I'm sorry to hear about Quan. Loke too. I know y'all loved them. It's fucked up what they did to y'all. Shit to us. But we all walked away with our lives, so anything else ain't shit. This baby is a blessing, Aspen. Even if that sorry ass nigga had a part in making it. And I for one am gonna be the best auntie I can possibly be," Justice continued.

"Me too. This baby 'bout to be so spoiled," Brianna agreed, wrapping her arm around Aspen's shoulders.

"Thanks y'all. I love y'all," Aspen cried.

"We love you too," Justice replied.

"In real life though y'all, I just don't understand how I didn't see what Quan was doing. That nigga really played a role for two whole years. That shit fuckin' me up," Aspen revealed.

"Yeah, me too. I thought Loke really loved me. Nobody

could have paid me enough to ever believe he would do me like this. I really loved that man y'all. And now he's gone, and I don't even know how to feel about it," Brianna confessed.

"Awww, I'm so sorry y'all. And I know it's hard, but them niggas wasn't shit. They was sent to lead us to death, and I'm just glad that shit didn't work."

CHAPTER SEVENTEEN

It was three weeks before Aspen's due date, and Justice and Brianna had put together a baby shower. She'd found out that she was having a boy, so when she walked into the *Toy Story* themed event, she was taken aback. Her best friends had spared no expense in planning the party, and Aspen couldn't have been happier. Everything was put together perfectly with nothing missing or out of place. There was a huge Buzz Light-year cake with mini cupcakes with Woody's face on them. There were giant pictures of all the *Toy Story* characters all around the room.

"Aspen, you look so beautiful," Shanté complimented before giving Aspen a hug.

"Thank you, Ms. Shanté. I feel fat as hell."

"Girl, you're not fat. You're carrying my grandchild. This just proves that he's gonna be a healthy baby."

"Alright nah, Ms. Shanté, you better speak. All I want is a healthy baby," Aspen replied.

Aspen wore a long, light blue dress with white gold accessories that set the look off. Her makeup was professionally done, and her bob was curled to perfection. She looked beautiful as she sat in a huge blue and gold chair in the front of the room. Behind her head was a huge sign that read "Baby Dallas", and she'd never felt more loved.

"Aspen, let's get some pictures of you in the chair before you start opening your gifts," Justice suggested.

Aspen agreed and began posing for the pictures. She was all smiles, and she thanked her friends for the beautiful baby shower they hosted. It really meant a lot to her, and she was sure they didn't know how much. They had been by her side during the entire pregnancy, and she couldn't ask for better friends. Justice and Brianna began handing her gift after gift, and she opened them one by one, holding each one up so they all could see what she'd received.

"Y'all it's so much stuff. This baby ain't even here yet, and y'all already got him spoiled rotten." Aspen laughed.

"He's not spoiled; he's just well loved," Brianna corrected.

"Right! Bitch, if you think this is spoiled, you ain't seen nothing yet. He for damn sure can get whatever he wants from Auntie Justice."

"Aww, I love y'all," Aspen uttered.

"We love you too," Brianna replied.

Aspen had been opening gifts for the last twenty minutes,

and there was still a pile of gifts left. She didn't even know how she was going to get everything back to her house. She looked around at all the gifts, thinking that she would need to rent a small U-Haul to get everything back to her home.

"It's still so much for me to open. But I got to go to the bathroom first. This little boy is laying on my bladder," Aspen announced, standing to her feet. As soon as she stood up, she felt a pop, and water began flowing from between her legs.

"Aspen, I know yo ass didn't just pee on yourself in front of everybody?" Brianna questioned.

"Girl, her fucking water broke," Justice called out as she rushed over to Aspen's side. "We gotta get you to the hospital," Justice continued, helping Aspen out of the room and to her car. Brianna and Shanté were close behind, eager to see Aspen become a mother.

They made their way to the hospital, and Aspen was taken into a room immediately. Before her water broke, she was feeling slight pains in her stomach, but they were so mild that she didn't think anything of it. However, as she laid in that hospital bed, she screamed for the doctors to give her pain medicine.

"Once he gets here, it's gonna be all worth it," Brianna assured.

"Well, can he hurry up and get here because this shit hurts? Where the fuck is the doctors with my damn epidural?" Aspen yelled.

She felt like her body was being ripped in half, and

nothing she did eased the pain. She didn't understand how any woman could go through this type of pain without the help of medication. She laid on her side, griping the bed rail and rocking herself back-and-forth.

"They coming, Aspen. They said they had to page the anesthesiologist. Just give him time to get here," Justice reminded.

"That's easy for you to say. You not the one laying here with an entire human trying to come out your body. This fuckin' shit hurts like hell. I need them to hurry up."

A few moments later, the nurse walked inside the room. She went to the sink and washed her hands before placing gloves onto them.

"I'm here to check your cervix," she informed.

"Where is the anesthesiologist?" Aspen asked. "I'm in a lot of pain, and it's very uncomfortable. I need that epidural."

"He's coming. He wants to see how dilated you are, and then he will be right in," the nurse informed.

Aspen nodded her head, and the nurse walked over to her. Aspen turned onto her back and opened her legs. The uncomfortableness of the nurse checking her cervix caused her to let out a heavy breath. She closed her eyes, and tears fell from them.

"Oh, my God, that was fast. Ms. Billups, you're at nine centimeters. I have to get the doctor in here now," she informed.

"Good, get somebody in here to give me my epidural because this shit hurts."

"I don't think you understand, Ms. Billups. This baby is about to come. You're way too far along to get an epidural. This baby is coming," the nurse revealed before walking out the room.

"What does she mean? I can't have this baby naturally. I need medication. What does she mean it's too late? I been waiting on them," Aspen cried.

"Calm down, Aspen. Women have been having babies without medication since the beginning of time. Everything is going to be fine. You got this," Justice coached.

"No, the fuck I don't. I don't care what other women did; I need meds. I'm not strong enough for this shit. I can't do it y'all. I need an epidural. There is no way I can continue to take this pain."

Aspen was hysterical as tears poured from her eyes. She was terrified and had no clue of the real pain of childbirth. She'd heard women speak about how bad it hurt. However, to actually go through it hit different. Before Aspen knew it, the doctor was coming in, followed by two nurses. Aspen had no choice but to get ready once the nurse informed the doctor that she was ten centimeters dilated.

"Okay, Aspen, it's time for you to start pushing. Your friends are going to hold your legs back while I count down from ten. During that time, I want you to push as hard as you can. Ladies, I need you to get on opposite sides of her and hold her legs up," the doctor ordered. They both agreed, and Justice rushed to Aspen's left side. Once her legs were held back, the doctor began counting down from ten.

"Ahhhhhhh," Aspen screamed as she pushed. Once the doctor got to one, she leaned back in the bed and rested for a few seconds.

"Again, Aspen. Ten, nine, eight." The doctor counted.

Several pushes later, Aspen was tired, and her son was still inside her. She was becoming weak and knew she wouldn't be able to take the pain much longer. "I can't do it anymore. It hurts too bad," she cried. Her tears were mixing with her sweat, and it ran down her face.

"I know it's hard, Aspen, but you're doing a great job. You're so close. It's almost time to meet your son. Just a few more pushes," one of the nurses coached.

"On your next contraction, we're going to start pushing again," the doctor informed.

An exhausted Aspen nodded her head and prepared herself for her next contraction. When the doctor informed Aspen it was coming, he told her to push as hard as she could as soon as she started feeling it. Aspen agreed and started pushing as the doctor counted.

"The head is right here. It's almost in my hand. You're going to give me a big push on the next one."

Aspen nodded, and as soon as she felt the contraction coming on, she began pushing. Aspen pushed as hard as she could for those ten seconds, and when she was done, the doctor told her the head was out.

"He has so much hair. He's almost here, Aspen. You're doing amazing. Just a few more pushes," Justice guided, wiping sweat from Aspen's forehead.

Aspen pushed one more time, and then she heard her baby crying. "Awww, he's here!" Brianna cheered as she wiped tears from her eyes.

The nurse wiped the baby off before lying him on Aspen's chest. She cried as she looked down at her sweet baby boy. *I can't believe I did it. I'm somebody's mother,* she thought to herself. She vowed right then to protect him with her life and to be the best mother she could possibly be.

"Welcome to the world, Dallas Mario Billups," Aspen whispered, kissing her son on his forehead. At that moment, all her fears of motherhood went out the window. She knew they had each other and that everything would be okay.

"He is everything, Aspen," Justice complimented.

"Yes, he is," Aspen agreed.

Aspen had never been happier as she looked down at her newborn son. He was so beautiful, and she was so lucky to have him. The love of a child was unconditional and without reason, and that was exactly what Aspen needed. Her heart was so full of joy, and it was at that moment that she knew he was the one that saved her. Everything she'd done in life — good and bad — led Aspen to that moment — to be sitting there holding her newborn son. Now, she would spend the rest of her life showing Dallas gratitude for what he'd unknow-ingly done for her.

BOTH BRIANNA AND JUSTICE WERE AT THE HOSPITAL THE DAY Aspen was discharged. They were ready to get her home. They had planned a small welcome home dinner for Aspen and Dallas, which Shanté and Cream were putting the finishing touches on.

Aspen dressed Dallas in a red and black Nike outfit with a hat and socks to match. She was excited about being a mother and was ready to see where their life would take them. It was the two of them from here on out, them against the world. When the nurse walked in and handed Aspen her paperwork, they were ready to go. Aspen sat into the wheelchair as the nurse placed Dallas' car seat on her lap before wheeling her out of the room. Justice went and got her car from the parking lot, pulling it up to the front entrance. Brianna grabbed Dallas' car seat from Aspen's lap and secured it in Justice's backseat.

"You ready to go, Aspen?" Justice asked, looking into her rearview mirror once Aspen was in the backseat.

"Hell yeah! I been in that damn hospital for two days. My ass ready to get back home and be in my own damn bed. I got so sick of them people waking me up in the middle of the damn night, always wanting to check somethin'. They told me to sleep when the baby sleeps, but how the hell was I supposed to do that when every time we went to sleep, here they come waking him up? Get me far away from this damn place."

"I know that's right." Brianna laughed.

About fifteen minutes later, they were pulling up to Aspen's house. There were big blue letters on Aspen's lawn that spelled out the words, "Welcome Home Dallas," and all Aspen could do was smile.

"Awww, y'all are so sweet. Thank you." Aspen beamed.

"Girl, this is nothing. Let's go inside," Brianna suggested.

They all got out the car, and when Aspen walked inside, she was taken aback. There were blue, white, and silver balloons all around her home. A huge spread of lamb chops, lobster tails, crab legs, garlic mashed potatoes, asparagus, and salad was in her kitchen, along with a host of different desserts. Over in her living room was a pile of gifts, and tears formed in Aspen's eyes.

"Welcome home, Aspen," Shanté cheered, grabbing Dallas' car seat from Brianna.

"Awww, y'all didn't have to do all this." Aspen smiled.

"Yes, we did. You just brought my nephew into this world. I know you didn't think we was just gonna do nothing for you. You should have known it was gon' be up for you when you got out that hospital. Y'all remember what y'all did for me after I got shot?" Justice reminded, referring to the huge party they threw her when she got out of the hospital.

"You deserve this, Aspen. We 'bout to eat some good food,

and then you gon' open all your push gifts," Brianna announced.

"Thank y'all," Aspen cooed.

Shanté placed Dallas into the bassinet in the living room. It was one of the three that was inside the home. They all joined around the dining room table, preparing to eat. Cream said grace before they all made their plates.

"This is so sweet y'all. Thank y'all for doing this," Aspen expressed.

"Girl, you don't have to keep thanking us. You know we got you. We're your village," Brianna assured as she dipped her crab leg into butter.

When they were finished eating, they all went into the living room so that Aspen could open her gifts. She was so excited to be so loved. She was thankful for the family she had in the people in front of her. She sat down in a chair and was handed her first gift.

Here, Aspen, this gift is from me. I want you to open this one first before you start getting to all the expensive shit they bought you," Shanté joked.

Aspen laughed as she grabbed the huge gift box. Inside the box was a huge picture Shanté had gotten painted of Aspen, Cove, and their mother and father. She had used one of the pictures from the baby shower, being sure to show off Aspen's pregnant belly. It instantly brought tears to Aspen's eyes.

"Ms. Shanté, thank you so much. This is the most beautiful

gift I've ever received. I'm gonna hang it up right here in the living room," Aspen declared, pointing over to the wall.

"You're welcome. I wanted to get you something that would be dear to your heart, and I noticed that you don't have any pictures of you all together," Shante announced.

"You got a hammer and some nails? I can hang it up right now," Cream suggested. Aspen told him where everything was located before she was handed another gift.

"I got you two but open this one first," Brianna suggested, handing her one of the two Louis Vuitton gift bags that sat on the floor.

"Awww, shit, I'm excited!" Aspen beamed, pulling the huge orange box from the gift bag. When she opened the box, she saw the pink and yellow Neverfull bag she'd been wanting to get. Her smile brightened as she thanked her. Brianna handed her the next bag and inside was the shoes to match.

"Girl, you know me too well. I was just lookin' at these shoes and bag online."

"I got the bag in blue." Brianna giggled.

Aspen continued to open her gifts and thanked everyone for everything they bought her. She felt so loved in that moment that she didn't even miss not having her child's father around to share it with. Her friends truly were her village, and she was beyond grateful for them. Dallas began fussing, and Aspen knew it was time for him to eat.

"I'll get him. You just rest. You have many sleepless nights ahead of you. Let Grandma Shanté get this one."

"Thank you." Aspen smiled.

They sat and gushed over little Dallas for a few more hours. Letting Aspen know that she could call them if she needed anything, they all walked out the door, leaving Aspen and Dallas alone.

"It's just me and you now, little guy. It might be like this a lot but just know Mommy got you," Aspen whispered to Dallas. She sat there, looking into his tiny face, and all she saw was Quan. Dallas looked just like him, and Aspen couldn't help but wonder what would have happened if Quan was alive. If he'd never set her up, would they be a family? Would they be cuddled up on the couch while enjoying their newborn son? Just the thought brought a tear to her eyes.

"I wonder if things would have gone differently if I would have told Quan I was pregnant," Aspen said aloud. As much as she wanted to know the answer to that question, she knew it was something she would never know. Shanté had already put all the food up, so Aspen took Dallas upstairs to her room where they spent the rest of the night.

EPILOGUE

Five Years Later

Aspen brought a bowl of potato salad out to one of the picnic tables in her backyard. Cream was on the grill grilling slabs of ribs along with chicken wings, hot dogs, and burgers. Brianna was filling the coolers with ice and different drinks, while Justice was placing Dallas' cake onto a serving tray. It was his fifth birthday, and Aspen couldn't believe how fast the time had gone by. She felt like she'd just had Dallas yesterday, and now he was turning five. He sat, playing in the yard with Justice and Cream's three-year-old son, Kingston, as they waited for the rest of the partygoers to arrive. Aspen had passed out invitations to a few of the children in Dallas' kindergarten class, and seven of them had RSVP'd.

Aspen had hired a clown and a magician to perform at the party, as well as a DJ to keep the music going for as long as the party lasted. Aspen wanted to give Dallas a fifth birthday party that he would always remember. She could tell he was having fun and enjoying himself, and that was all she wanted.

"Mommy, when are we going to eat cake and ice cream? I love cake and ice cream," Dallas asked, staring up at her as he blinked his huge, gray eyes. Aspen had passed down her beautiful gray eyes to her son. They were the same gray eyes that were passed down to her from her mother.

"We have to wait until your friends get here, so we can sing happy birthday. But before we do that, we have to eat the food that me and Uncle Cream made," Aspen replied.

"I'm hungry now. Can I have some ribs, baked beans, and macaroni?" Dallas asked.

"Yeah, give me a second. Your friends will be here in a minute, so let me finish setting this food out. Then once I'm done, I'll make you and Kingston a plate."

"Okay, Mommy," Dallas replied before running back over to play with Kingston.

Several moments later, Dallas' friends began to arrive. Aspen showed them into the backyard where the party was being held. "Please help yourselves to the food. Everything you need is over on the table," Aspen called out, picking up two plates, one for Dallas and the other for Kingston.

Everyone sat around, eating barbecue and enjoying a few laughs. When everyone was finished eating, the clown came out, putting on a show for the children, while the adults enjoyed a few beverages.

"This is such a nice party, Aspen. These children are having so much fun," Tamar complimented. She was the mother of Dallas' friend, Joshua

"Thanks, girl. I hope Josh is enjoying himself."

"Girl, look at him. He can't get enough of that clown." She laughed.

Aspen looked over to find Joshua standing in the clown's face. He was practically forcing her to make him all the different balloon animals there were in a zoo. Aspen couldn't help but to laugh as she felt sorry for the poor clown. After the magician finished his magic show, it was time to sing happy birthday.

QUAN STOOD, WATCHING ALL THE PEOPLE SING HAPPY birthday to his son, a son that he'd never even met before. Every day he'd beat himself up for the way he'd betrayed Aspen. He knew he'd wronged her, and there were no words that could explain how sorry he was. He felt like they were better off thinking he was dead, so Quan continued to allow them to think just that.

He'd asked himself everyday why he agreed to Lashay's plan. If he would have never met up with her that day, none of this would have happened. At first, he didn't know Aspen, so it didn't matter to him. Lashay had offered him twenty thousand dollars to pretend to like her and then find out everything he could on her. Although he'd started to catch feelings for Aspen, the fifty thousand Lashay promised them for bringing Aspen and Brianna to her was something he couldn't pass up. However, if he would have known Aspen was pregnant, he would have never agreed.

Looking at his son's smiling face as he looked up at Aspen let Quan know he'd played himself. He'd played himself out of ever knowing the love of a family he created and the bond of a father and his first-born son. He wanted to run to Aspen and beg for her to forgive him, but he knew what would come of that. He didn't want to cause Aspen any more hurt than he already had, so he continued to allow them to think he was dead.

He'd indeed been shot, but instead of dying, he had lived. He was hit in the side, but the bullet had gone straight through. When he was hit, he didn't move an inch, no matter how much the bullet hole hurt, knowing that if he let them know he was alive, they would kill him without hesitation. Quan had been the only one that survived, and he was grateful. However, he knew all of this was his own fault.

Thinking back on that day, he thought about lying on the cold basement floor, praying for God to spare his life. There were so many gunshots happening around him, and they were dropping the bodies of everyone in his crew. The moment he heard the footsteps running up the stairs and out the house, Quan felt relief. Quan got up, looking around at the bodies that lay spread out on the floor. All he could do was shake his head because they never thought this would be the outcome of their plan. Quan left the house quickly before any police arrived.

Quan tried his best to stay away from Aspen, but he couldn't. He hadn't realized how much he loved her until it was too late. Quan knew that nothing he could say or do would ever make Aspen believe that, and he knew that was his fault. He couldn't blame her for hating him, so he didn't. One day, as he sat in his car, he couldn't keep Aspen off his mind, so he decided to pay her a visit. He wouldn't let himself be seen, but he just wanted to see how she was doing. So, he decided to take a ride over to her house.

When he pulled up, he parked across the street, a bit farther down from her house so he wouldn't be noticed. It had been about seven months since the day they handed the girls over to Lashay, and Quan missed Aspen. She'd just pulled into her driveway and got out the car when Quan noticed her pregnant belly, and it took his breath away. Suddenly, everything began to come back to him.

Aspen was supposed to give Justice her kidney that day, but she didn't. She never told me the reason why she didn't give it to her, but now I see why. Aspen was pregnant. She's about to have my baby, Quan thought to himself. A tear came to his eye when he realized he was about to get his own child killed.

"How could I have been so stupid? The one woman that truly loved me is the one I fuck over. And for what? Some money that I didn't even get. Aspen gave me a family, and I couldn't even be there for that," Quan said aloud to himself. All he could do was shake his head at the way he'd allowed such an unstable individual to dictate his life. He knew he wouldn't be able to get too close to them, but he vowed to keep an eye on them and make sure they were always okay.

So, every year since Dallas was born, Quan would check on them three times a year — once on Dallas' birthday, once on Aspen's birthday, and the last time on Christmas. He wanted so badly to let them know that he was still alive. He wanted to plead his case to Aspen and beg for her to take him back. However, his pride wouldn't allow him to take the rejection he knew he would receive. So, instead, he watched from the sideline as his son opened the birthday gifts he'd received, not one of them being from Quan. He stood there, watching the entire party without anyone even knowing it. He didn't leave until the entire party was over, and everyone had left.

ASPEN HAD JUST COME DOWNSTAIRS FROM TUCKING DALLAS in, and now it was time to clean up. Cream had already left to take Kingston home, while Justice and Brianna stayed behind to help Aspen clean.

"So, are you ready for Cove to come home tomorrow?"

Justice asked as she sprayed cleaning solution onto the kitchen counters.

"Hell yeah! I'm waking up early to make sure I'm sitting right there when them gates open," Aspen informed.

"I know that's right. She been gone way too long," Brianna stated.

"Shit, if it wasn't for her getting out early for good behavior, she would still be in there. But I'm so glad that my sister is finally coming home."

"Me too," Justice agreed. "Is everything all set for her welcome home party this weekend? If you need me to do anything, just let me know."

"Yep, everything is together. The decorator and her team are going to the hall Saturday morning to decorate. All we gotta do is be there Saturday night and party like rock stars," Aspen replied. It had been years since her sister had been home, and Aspen was ready to pick right back up where she left off.

Aspen had kept her sister's house even though she had bought her own a couple years back. She'd also put away money for Cove for when she was released. Aspen made sure her sister was good the same way Cove made sure Aspen was good.

"I know she gon' be excited to be home and to finally get to meet Dallas," Brianna expressed.

"Yeah, I can't wait to see how they interact. I already know they gon' have an unbreakable bond."

"Oh, you already know. Cove gon' love that baby like it was her own," Justice agreed.

Once they were done cleaning, Aspen opened a bottle of wine, pouring each a glass before they made their way to the living room. The three friends were amazed at how far they'd come. They'd faced things that would have broken a normal person, and they'd still come out on top. No matter what life threw at them, they faced it together and got through it together. Not even blood could make them closer.

"Aspen, is it cool if I just crash here for the night? It's already late. I gotta come here early tomorrow morning anyway to watch Dallas when you go pick up Cove. So, I just might as well spend the night," Brianna questioned.

"Girl, you know you don't even have to ask that. You know exactly where my guest room is."

"Thank you, girl," Brianna replied, taking off her shoes to get more comfortable.

"Them kids enjoyed the hell outta that party. I already know Kingston gon' be knocked out when I get home. And shit, as tired as I am, I won't be too far behind him," Justice spoke.

She finished her wine before hugging both Aspen and Brianna and walking out the door. Not soon after, Aspen made her way up to her room while Brianna went inside the guest room, both falling asleep the moment their heads hit the pillow.

. . .

THE NEXT MORNING, ASPEN WOKE UP BRIGHT AND EARLY, getting right in the shower. She did her hair before getting dressed. When she was done, she went inside Dallas' room to check on him. He was still sound asleep. Aspen walked over to him, kissing him gently on his forehead before walking out the room. Before she left, she walked into her guest room to wake Brianna up and let her know she was leaving.

"Okay, girl. I'll see you when you get back," Brianna replied.

Aspen got into her car and made her way to the prison to pick up her sister. Aspen drove with the windows down as she made her way to Huron Valley. She sang along to Sza as she drove down the highway, eager to see her sister. Cove had been locked up for ten years, and Aspen couldn't wait to get her all caught up on all the newest music and fashion. Most importantly, she couldn't wait for Cove to meet Dallas.

She pulled up to the prison fifteen minutes before nine. Cove wasn't scheduled to be released until nine thirty that morning; however, Aspen was so excited that she wanted to arrive early. She and Dallas had made a welcome home sign for Cove, which Aspen planned to be holding up when the gates opened.

At nine-twenty-eight, Aspen got out of her car and retrieved the sign from her trunk. She walked through the parking lot and up to the gate, ready to see her sister's smiling face. As soon as the gates started to open, Aspen held up the sign. The moment she saw Cove, tears began falling from her eyes. She'd missed her sister so much that it was overwhelming. They ran to one another, hugging each other tightly as they both cried.

"Cove, I can't believe you're finally out." Aspen beamed, still holding her sister close.

"Well, believe it, girl, cause I'm right here."

"Girl, I can't wait for you to meet Dallas. He's so excited. He helped me make this sign for you."

"I can tell by the cute little stick figures on the bottom," Cove joked.

"Yeah, he said they were the three of us." Aspen laughed. "Where do you want to go first?" Aspen asked her.

"Home so that I can take a real shower and put on some real clothes," Cove suggested, looking down at her gray sweets. Cove had gained about thirty pounds since she'd been in prison. Although the extra weight looked good on her, she could no long fit the clothes she came in with, so she had to wear a pair of prison sweats for her release.

"I got you, sis, get in."

Aspen and Cove stepped into Aspen's white Range Rover and left the prison, never looking back. Cove rolled the passenger window down, closing her eyes as the air hit her face. She took in a deep breath of the fresh air, smiling as she let it out. She was finally free, and at twenty-nine, she planned to make the most of her life. She'd done the time for her sister, and she didn't regret that. However, the rest of her life was hers, and she was going to live it to the fullest.

"Whose house is this?" Cove asked as Aspen parked her car in the driveway.

"This is my house. I can take you home if you want, but Dallas is here."

"No, I can go home later. I just didn't know you moved, and we no longer lived together. I thought I was going to be an in-home auntie," Cove joked.

They both got out the car, and the smell of breakfast hit them as soon as they opened the door. Brianna had cooked an entire spread, and Cove's stomach growled the moment she smelled it.

"Y'all right on time. I just finished cooking."

"Girl, I didn't know you were gonna do all this. I planned to take her out to eat," Aspen stated.

"Well, now you don't have to. Welcome home, Cove," Brianna said as she walked around the kitchen island to hug Cove.

"Thank you, Bri. I'm happy to be home. Where's my little nephew?"

"He's upstairs playing with his toys."

"I'll go get him," Aspen offered.

Aspen walked up the stairs, and when she came back down, she was accompanied by the most handsome little boy Cove had ever seen. She walked to them, getting on her knees, so they could be eye level.

"Hey, handsome man. I'm your Auntie Cove, and I love you very much. I know you don't really know me, but I plan to make up for all the time we lost, and before you know it, we gonna be best friends."

"I know you. Mommy talks about you all the time. And I know you love me. I love you too. Me and Mommy pray for you every night," Dallas revealed.

Cove looked up at Aspen with tears in her eyes before hugging Dallas. She was so glad to be home and around the love of her family.

"Can we eat now, Mommy? I'm hungry. Auntie Bri took a long time to make the food."

"Sure, we can eat. Go sit at your table and I'll make your plate," Aspen suggested.

Walking into the kitchen, Aspen grabbed Dallas' red *Paw Patrol* plate and began placing waffles, eggs, hash browns, sausage, and bacon onto it before bringing the plate to Dallas. Walking back into the kitchen, she poured orange juice into his matching cup and brought that to him as well. Once Dallas was all set, it was time for Aspen to make her own plate. Brianna and Cove were already in the kitchen, piling food onto their plates, and Aspen joined them. The girls walked into the dining room where they sat at the table.

"Cove, I made you a hair and nail appointment for Thursday," Aspen informed.

"Good cause I need this shit done bad. I'm sick of this damn ponytail. Why Thursday though? They didn't have any closer appointments?"

"They did, but I wanted the shit to be freshly done for your welcome home party on Friday," Aspen replied.

"What party?"

"The party I been planning for you. It's gon' be lit, sista. We gon' have so much fun."

"Sista, you didn't have to do that, but I'm glad you did." Cove laughed.

Once they were all done eating, Aspen showed Cove to the bathroom before handing her everything she would need to take a shower. She then headed back downstairs with Brianna and Dallas. She'd just sat on the couch when her cell phone rang. She looked down at it to see a number that she didn't know. Not thinking anything of it, Aspen answered her phone. When she didn't hear anyone else on the other end, she repeated herself.

"Hello?" she said again. Without saying anything, the caller hung up. Aspen shrugged it off, thinking it was a wrong number, before placing her phone onto her coffee table.

"Alright, Aspen, I'm gonna get outta here and get back home. I'm gonna give you some time alone with your sister," Brianna said.

"Okay, I'ma call you a little later. Thanks for everything, Bri."

"Girl, you know I got you. I'll talk to you later," she announced before walking out the door.

"Mommy, can we watch *Sonic*?" Dallas asked, walking into the living room.

"Just for a second. We have to get you dressed so that we can take Auntie Cove shopping."

"Can I get some toys when we go shopping?"

"Yeah, Mommy will get you some toys, baby boy. And okay, just one episode then we have to get you dressed," Aspen agreed, grabbing the remote and turning on Dallas' favorite show.

When it was over, Aspen took him upstairs to get dressed. Once everyone was ready to go, they made their way to Aspen's Rover and headed to Sommerset Mall. Before they got out the car, Aspen reached inside her purse and handed Cove a Chase bank card.

"What's this?" Cove asked in confusion.

"It's your bank card. I wanted to make sure you had an account when you came home. I been saving for you," Aspen revealed.

"Damn, for real, sis? That's dope. Thank you. How much on it?"

"More than enough for you to go in here and tear this place down and still have hella bands left over," Aspen joked.

"Bitch, for real?" Cove said with wide eyes.

"They got an ATM inside; you can check your balance. The pin is your birthday, but you can change it if you want to."

Once inside, the first thing Cove did was find an ATM. She needed an entire wardrobe but needed to know exactly how much she was working with. Sliding her card into the slot, she punched in her pin number before hitting the check balance button. When the screen read two hundred and fifty thousand dollars, her mouth dropped open. She looked over at her sister in disbelief.

"Aspen, I don't know what to say."

"It's nothing to say, sis. I got you," Aspen replied.

"Thank you," Cove whispered.

They walked around the mall, looking for the first phone store they saw. Cove didn't give a damn about the provider. She just needed a phone. They walked into a T-Mobile store, and Cove purchased an iPhone 15 and immediately gave her new number to Aspen. They walked through the mall, stopping in store after store, buying anything they wanted. Cove had so many bags they had to put them inside the car before walking back into the mall. When they were finally finished shopping, Aspen suggested they stop at Walmart to get Cove any hygiene products that she might need.

"Yayyyy, I wanna go to Walmart. They got lots of toys there," Dallas cheered.

"That's right, baby, and you can get whatever toys you want," Cove assured.

"Girl, that boy has enough toys. Don't spend your money on toys for him. That money is for you. I'll let him pick out two toys, and I'll buy them," Aspen informed.

"Bitch, bye. That's my nephew, and I ain't been around. I got some birthdays and Christmases to make up for. In fact, lil' dude just had a birthday. So, like I said, he can get whatever he wants," Cove countered.

Aspen laughed as she shook her head. They pulled up inside the Walmart parking lot, and Aspen's phone began to ring. She parked and grabbed her phone, but it stopped ringing before she could get to it. Noticing the number was the same number that called her earlier, she put her phone back inside her purse, and they all got out the car. After getting all the products Cove would need, with Aspen picking up a few things as well, they made their way to the toy aisle. Dallas picked out every toy he wanted, and Cove allowed him to put it in the basket before they walked to the register.

"Y'all hungry? All this shopping done made me work up an appetite. I think we need food," Aspen suggested.

"I'm hungry," Dallas called out as Aspen placed him into the backseat.

"Yeah, me too. What y'all want to eat?" Cove asked.

"What do you want to eat is the real question. You the one that's been eating that nasty ass food all this time. So, it's whatever you want, sis. I can cook, we can go out to eat, or we can Door Dash some food and chill at my house."

"You mean like get Chinese food and watch movies?" Cove questioned, looking up at Aspen.

"Hell yeah, if that's what you want. It's your world, sis. I'm just living in it."

Aspen pulled out the parking lot and headed back to her house. After bringing all the bags inside, Aspen ordered the food before they all took showers and changed into their pajamas. Aspen was happy to have her sister home. The emptiness she'd felt from not having her around was finally filled, and Aspen couldn't have asked for anything better. When the food arrived, Aspen made their plates while Cove brought Dallas' table into the living room so that he could eat with them while they watched movies.

"Dallas, you pick the first movie," Cove suggested.

"Okay, let's watch *Leo*. It's on Netflix."

Aspen nodded her head and turned on the movie. They watched it while they ate, and when they were finished eating, Dallas came and joined them on the couch. They spent the rest of the night watching movies, not going to sleep until well into the night. Cove went back to her house the next morning, letting Aspen know she would be back over Thursday for her hair and nail appointment.

THE DAY OF COVE'S PARTY CAME QUICKLY, AND EVERYTHING was ready. Ms. Shanté had offered to babysit Dallas during the party, and Aspen was on her way to drop him off. On her way back to her home to get dressed, her cell phone rang. She answered it and heard nothing on the other end. She knew it was the same number that had been calling her, and she didn't understand what they wanted.

"Why do you keep calling me if you're not going to say shit? We too old to be playing on phones!" Aspen yelled. When the person still didn't say anything, Aspen yelled out a fuck you before ending the call.

When Aspen got home, Cove was parked in her driveway, waiting on her.

"Hey, sista, what you doing here?" Aspen asked as she got out of the car.

"I just wanted to get dressed over here and ride to the party together. We can have a few drinks and listen to some music while we get dressed," Cover suggested.

"Cool with me. I just need to eat a little something first before I start drinking."

"I know that's right. I need a little sandwich or something," Cove joked.

Walking into Aspen's house, they walked into the kitchen, and Aspen began pulling things out of the fridge to make a sandwich. "Yep, this all I need right here. This gon' hold me over til I eat at the party," Cove spoke, referring to the sandwich.

Once they were done eating, Aspen made them both a drink before they headed upstairs to begin getting dressed. Aspen turned on some music, and they jammed to Sexyy Redd as they applied their makeup. They dressed to the nines with Aspen wearing a black Chanel mini dress with a pair of platform Dolce and Gabbana cheetah print sling backs. A black Chanel bucket bag graced her shoulder, and her fragrance of choice was Kilian's Love Don't Be Shy. She looked good and smelled even better.

Cove equally matched Aspen's fly, wearing a red Chanel one piece with a gold Jacquemus handbag and gold Chanel heels. Her fragrance of choice was Gentle Fluidity Gold, and she felt like a bag of money.

"Damn, we look good! Let's take a picture," Cove suggested. They both posed, taking a selfie before they felt the house, making their way to what Aspen knew would be a night to remember.

Cove and Aspen arrived at the venue about twenty minutes later, noticing that people were already starting to arrive. They parked their car and got out, walking inside the building. The party was already lit as the DJ bumped Nicki Minaj's *Fuck Da Club Up.* They walked through the crowd, headed to the VIP area. Much to their surprise, Brianna, Justice, and Cream were already sitting at the table with a few bottles and a platter of hot wings.

"There goes the woman of the hour," Brianna announced, watching Cove and Aspen walking over to them.

"Girl, you look good as hell. My ass bought my body, but I see all I had to do was get locked up," Justice joked.

"Yeah, this ass is a little phat," Cove said, turning around in circles playfully. They took their seats at the booth and poured themselves some drinks. Everyone walked up to Cove, welcoming her home and handing her envelopes of money. She felt like hood royalty as everyone showed her love. As soon as the house music came on, Brianna made her way to the dance floor right along with Cove. The girls were having a time, and they were loving every minute of it. Cove hadn't had this much fun in years, and she had her sister to thank for it all.

The party went on until well after two, and by the time they made their way back to Aspen's house, the sun was on its way up. They pulled into Aspen's driveway and drunkenly walked into the house.

"That party was everything, sista. I had so much fun. And the food was good as hell. The lamb chops still got my mouth watering. Who did you have cater it? I'ma need to hire they asses myself," Cove questioned.

"This chef named Malone. He's dope. He does a lot of events around the city. I'll give you his Instagram.

"Bitch, I'm drunk as fuck," Aspen continued.

"Me too. I ain't drank like this in over ten years." Cove laughed.

Aspen was just about to tell Cove she was going to bed when her cell phone rang. Looking down at it, she saw it was the same number that had been calling her for the past few days. They never said anything, only held the phone, so Aspen decided not to answer, swiping the decline button. When they called right back, she decided to block the number. She was tired of whoever it was playing on her phone, so she was going to put it to an end. Heading up to her room, Aspen took a quick shower before getting into the bed.

The next morning, Aspen woke up to Cove in the living room, watching TV. She had a plate of food in her hand that she was eating, and Aspen instantly got hungry. Cove's eyes were glued to the TV as she watched old episodes of *My Wife and Kids.*

"Hey, sista, how you feeling this morning?" Aspen asked.

"I'm good. I thought I would be hungover from the way I was drinking last night, but I feel good. I ordered us some food. Yours is in the kitchen."

"Thank you." Aspen smiled as she made her way to the kitchen. A few moments later, she was making her way back to the living room with her plate. She sat on her couch and watched the TV with her sister.

"What you got up for the day?" Cove asked, dipping her chicken wing into a cup of ranch dressing.

"I gotta go get Dallas from Ms. Shanté house. I'ma go do that once I finish eating. After that, nothing. I think I'ma just chill for the rest of the day."

"Yeah, I feel you on that. I'ma go with you to pick up Dallas, just to see my lil' man. But after that, I'm taking my ass home. I got a date with my bed and Netflix." Cove laughed.

"I know that's right, girl."

Once they were done eating, Aspen showered before changing into a pair of light blue Off White sweats. She put on a matching Off White fitted cap and a pair of black Gucci sunglasses. After that, she was ready to go. When they made it to Shanté's house, Dallas was already packed and ready to go.

"Did you have fun with Grandma Shanté?" Aspen asked once she and Cove walked through the door.

"Yeah, we watched this show called *In Livin' Color*. It's a clown on there called Homie, and he don't play dat," Dallas cheered. "Can we get Homie for my next birthday party?" Dallas asked.

"Yeah, um, I don't know about all that, Dallas. Your birthday ain't until next year anyway. I'm sure you will want someone else there by then." Aspen laughed.

"Not Homie the clown." Cove laughed.

"Hey, Cove, welcome home, baby. I'm so glad to see you," Shanté announced, walking up to Cove and giving her a hug.

"Thank you, Shanté. I'm happy to be home."

"Well, Shanté, I don't mean to cut this visit short, but I gotta get outta here. We had a time last night, and I'm just ready to get home and be lazy," Aspen joked.

"You go ahead and do that. I'll see y'all later." Shanté watched as the three of them got into the car before she locked her door.

"Auntie Cove, can you watch *Sonic* with me tonight?" Dallas asked.

"Auntie Cove is tired, baby. How 'bout y'all watch *Sonic* another time?" Aspen suggested.

"Awww, but I wanna watch *Sonic* with Auntie Cove tonight. I haven't seen her in like so many nights," Dallas whined.

"It's only been one night. You spent one night at Grandma Shanté's house." Aspen laughed.

"Look, if my nephew wants to watch *Sonic* with me then

that's what we gon' do. I'll go home after that," Cove informed.

When they got back home, Dallas took Cove right into the living room to watch *Sonic*. Aspen couldn't help but smile at the beautiful relationship Dallas had with Cove. It was like she'd always been there because the love was unmatched. Aspen walked upstairs to her room. She wanted to give Dallas and Cove their time. They didn't even notice she was gone as they settled into the auntie/nephew date. Aspen had just gotten into her room when her cell phone rang. She looked down at it to see a number she didn't recognize, but she answered it anyway.

"Hello?" she spoke.

"You thought you could just get rid of me by blocking my number? Nah, bitch, I ain't going nowhere," a deep baritone spoke into the phone.

"Who the fuck is this?" Aspen asked.

"Oh, so I guess you don't know my fucking voice? I guess I can't get too mad. It has been years. But I remember you and what you did. Bitch, I'm here to introduce yo ass to a bitch called Karma."

"What the fuck are you talking 'bout? Either tell me who the fuck you are or I'm hanging up. I'm way too grown to be playing childish games," Aspen replied in a no-nonsense tone.

"Well, bitch, I didn't have much of a childhood. You took that shit away from us."

"Us? Who the fuck is us, and what the fuck you want? This shit is getting on my nerves."

"It's a shame you don't know your own cousin's voice. I guess that's to be expected though. You ruined my life, Aspen. You and yo bitch ass sister, Cove. Y'all killed my mama and had me and Marcus in and out of foster homes. Now it's your turn. I wonder if lil Dallas is strong enough to be in the system?"

With those words, Aspen's eyes widened. She hadn't spoken to Phillip in years, and now there he was. *How does he know my son's name? How did he get my number? Oh, my God, what if he knows where I live?* A million and one thoughts ran through Aspen's head at once as fear set in. She thought about how her life had turned out after the murder of her parents, and she knew she didn't want her son to go through that.

"What do you want, Phillip?" Aspen asked.

"For you to be dead and for your son to suffer the same pain me and my brother suffered. I'm looking at the lil' nigga right now, sitting on the couch with Cove. What's this they watching? *Sonic*?"

With those words, Aspen shot down the stairs. Her heart was racing, and her hands were shaking. She was scared as hell and had no clue what her next move was going to be. Cove saw the way that Aspen was running around the house, closing all the curtains, and she jumped to her feet. She knew something was wrong by the terrified look on Aspen's face.

"What's wrong, sista? Why you look like you seen a ghost? And why the hell are you running around here closing curtains?" Cove asked.

"Phillip is out there somewhere, and he watching us. He just called me," Aspen informed frantically.

"Girl, who the hell is Phillip? Is that one of your ex-boyfriends or something?"

"Bitch, Rochelle's son!" Aspen yelled.

The look on Cove's face let Aspen know she was just as scared as she was. Cove opened her mouth to speak, but before she could say anything, there was a hard pounding on Aspen's front door. The two sisters looked at each other in fear, not knowing what to do.

To be continued…

ENJOYED THE READ?

Did you enjoy the read?
Let us know how much by leaving us a review on Amazon
and Goodreads.

OTHER BOOKS BY

<u>URBAN AINT DEAD</u>

Tales 4rm Da Dale

The Hottest Summer Ever

Hittin' Licks For The Holidays: Atlanta

Wet Dreams On Lockdown: The Nurse

How To Publish A Book From Prison

By **Elijah R. Freeman**

Despite The Odds

By **Juhnell Morgan**

Good Girls Gone Rogue

Good Girls Gone Rouge 2

By **Manny Black**

Hittaz

Hittaz 2

Hittaz 3

Hittaz 4

Coldhearted

By **Lou Garden Price, Sr.**

Charge It To The Game

Charge It To The Game 2

A Summer To Remember With My Hitta

Snatched Up By A Hitta

Santa Sent Me A Real One For Christmas

Wet Dreams on Lockdown: The Unit Manager

Thug Me The Right Way 2

Thug Me The Right Way 3

By **Nai**

A Setup For Revenge

Wet Dreams On Lockdown: The Librarian

By **Ashley Williams**

Ridin' For You

Ridin' For You, Too

Trickin' on a Heaux for Christmas: A BBW Love Story

Homie Hoppin' For The Holidays

Wet Dreams on Lockdown: The Female C.O

Letters Of His Love

By **Telia Teanna**

The State's Witness

The State's Witness 2

The State's Witness 3

This Time Won't You Save Me

By **Kyiris Ashley**

Stuck In The Trenches

Stuck In The Trenches 2

By **Huff Tha Great**

The Swipe

The Swipe 2

By **Toōla**

Melted the Heart of a Menace

Wet Dreams On Lockdown: Lieutenant Grace

By **P. Wise**

Merry Trapmas: Ice & Frost

By **Mia Sky**

Thug Me The Right Way

By **DiamondATL & Nai**

Atlantastan

By **Chris Green**

IN The Streetz

By **Tron Hill**

Wet Dreams on Lockdown: The Male C.O

By **Tamyra Griffin**

Wet Dreams On Lockdown: The Counselor

By **Paris Iman**

Wet Dreams On Lockdown: The Warden

By **Shawnice**

Wet Dreams On Lockdown: The Captain

By **TN Jones**

This Time Won't You Save Me 3
His Summer Side Piece
By **Kyiris Ashley**

Ridin' Forever
By **Telia Teanna**

Pretti & The Beast
By **P. Wise**

Atlantastan 2
By **Chris Green**

IN The Streetz 2
Tron Hill

BOOKS BY

URBAN AINT DEAD's C.E.O

<u>Elijah R. Freeman</u>

Triggadale

Triggadale 2

Triggadale 3

Tales 4rm Da Dale

The Hottest Summer Ever

Murda Was The Case

Murda Was The Case 2

Murda Was The Case 3

Hittin' Licks For The Holidays: Atlanta

Wet Dreams On Lockdown: The Nurse

How To Publish A Book From Prison